WEIRD HORROR

NO.1

WEIRD HORROR 1
October 2020

© Undertow Publications and
its contributors

PUBLISHER
Undertow Publications
1905 Faylee Crescent, Pickering
ON, L1V 2T3, Canada

Undertowpublications.com
WeirdHorrorMag@gmail.com

EDITOR
Michael Kelly

STORY PROOFREADER
Carolyn Macdonell

LAYOUT, Additional artwork
Nathaniel Winter-Hebert

OPINION
Simon Strantzas

COMMENTARY
Orrin Grey

BOOKS
Lysette Stevenson

FILMS
Tom Goldstein

COVER ART
Sam Heimer

**COVER AND
MASTHEAD DESIGN**
Vince Haig

INTERIOR ART
David Bowman

Welcome to the new pulp! **Weird Horror** magazine is a venue for fiction, articles, reviews, and commentary. Initially, we plan to publish twice yearly — March and October.

From October 1 through to November 30 we will be open to submissions of fiction. The best way to determine what we want is to pick up an issue.

FICTION GUIDELINES

Weird Horror magazine is open to submissions of fiction only from October 1 through November 30. The submission period covers 2 issues — March and October. Fiction must be original and previously unpublished anywhere, in any format, on any platform. Please do not query about reprints.

As we'll be reading for 2 issues, it may take the full submission period to respond. Simultaneous submissions are welcome.

Please inform us if your story is accepted elsewhere. No multiple submissions. Please send 1 story.

We are actively seeking new and underrepresented voices. We accept submissions from anyone, regardless of race, gender, or sexuality.

As our title suggests, we are seeking pulpy dark fiction in the weird fiction and horror genres of 500 to 5,000 words. Monsters, ghosts, creatures, fiends, demons, etc. Dark crime. Suspense. Mutants. Killers. Ghouls. Golems. Witches. Pulpy goodness! We are hoping to bring some fun (and terror) to our readers.

Payment is 1-cent-per-word (paid via PayPal) for first worldwide English-language rights, for use in the print and eBook editions. We ask for a 6-month exclusivity. Copyright remains with the author, and a contract will be provided.

Submit stories in Standard Manuscript Format as a Word document or PDF, and e-mail as an attachment to: *WeirdHorrorMag@gmail.com*

Please format the subject line of your e-mail thusly: Submission - Story Title - Author Name

Please keep your cover letter short. Submissions sent outside the submission period will not be read.

Please query if you have any questions.

ADVERTISING

Get your unique brand in front of our unique readers!

A full-page ad is just $60 (U.S.) per insertion. A half-page ad is $40. Ad space is very limited. We reserve the right to refuse unsuitable material. Please contact us at *WeirdHorrorMag@gmail.com*.

Michael Kelly

Strange! Eerie! Uncanny! Macabre!

Number 1   Contents for October, 2020   Volume 1

BEST LEFT IN THE SHADOWS, Simon Strantzas On Horror ... 6

**KICKING OPEN DOORS TO LIGHT AND SHADOW:
THE CRESTWOOD HOUSE MONSTER BOOKS,**
Grey's Grotesqueries by Orrin Grey ... 8

KRAZY KRAX, by Naben Ruthnum ... 10

WHITE NOISE IN A WHITE ROOM, by Steve Duffy ... 16

THE DEVIL AND THE DIVINE, by Inna Effress ... 28

CHILDREN OF THE ROTTING STRAW, by Steve Toase ... 36

HER VOICE, UNMASKED, by Suzan Palumbo ... 42

YOU CAN'T SAVE THEM ALL, by Ian Rogers ... 50

THE NIGHT KINGDOM, by Shikhar Dixit ... 62

WHERE THE HOLLOW TREE WAITS, by John Langan ... 70

THE MACABRE READER, Book Reviews by Lysette Stevenson ... 74

ABERRANT VISIONS, Film Reviews by Tom Goldstein ... 77

Welcome to the new pulp! Weird Horror magazine is a venue for fiction, articles, reviews, and commentary. Published twice yearly — March and October.

OPINION

SIMON STRANTZAS ON HORROR

Best Left
in the Shadows

I F WE'RE GOING to talk about Horror, be it Weird Horror, Quiet Horror, Urban Horror, Psychological Horror, Gothic Horror, or whatever your favourite kind of Horror is, first we have to define it. Wait! Before you stop reading: listen, I get it. The idea of defining Horror has been done. Again and again. Over and over. Since before the World Fantasy Convention was a glimmer in anybody's eye, there were a bunch of people sitting in a circle asking: "What do you think Horror is?"

So, what is it? Beats me. Because Horror is just another in a long line of names for this sort of fiction, and the only people really tied to the name are people like me: folks who grew up during the great boom, when Horror was a popular marketing term used to describe what we were reading and writing. All those categories I rattled off a paragraph ago? They're all the same Horror. The only potentially worthwhile distinction, the only true separation of Horror into different things, is the differentiation between the *genre* of Horror, and the *lens* of horror.

In the first case, Horror is easy to define: it's a set of tropes that, when combined add a recognizable element to a story. Take one nuclear family, add one old house plus a death in the past, sprinkle in a curse and a bit of blood. Bake at 350°F for 20 minutes or until done.

The other kind of Horror, the lens of horror, is a bit harder to define because by its nature it's undefinable. By which I don't mean we can't come up with some sort of definition, but rather that its boundaries can't be so clearly mapped. Fiction written through the lens of horror is fiction that is not about tropes, but rather about intention. It's about exploring those things and feelings that society, as a whole, doesn't want to deal with. The fears and the jealousies and the prejudices that inform our daily lives, transformed by the magic of fiction into metaphorical creatures and forces born of another place. It's often interstitial, often forward thinking, looking for new ways to reflect the world back to us in a way we can understand, even if that understanding is only instinctual.

But, as I said, we call it all Horror because that's what we call it. If we were born twenty years earlier, we might call it ESP Fiction. If we were born twenty years later, we might call it Weird Fiction. It's all the same thing under different coats of paint. We either want something new and different, or comfortable and familiar. Or, often, something between.

Because the whole idea that anything is binary is a crock, right? Can we agree on that? Horror isn't strictly commercial, and it isn't strictly artistic. It doesn't just make you think, and it doesn't just make you feel. Good Horror, like good everything else, works in the grey areas between. How close you want to get to either extreme is the only question, and the answer doesn't always need to be the same.

But here's the thing: it's not just about knowing what you want. It's about knowing where to find it. Because not all venues are equal. The more you want the fiction you read to eschew tropes and be written through the lens of horror, the more you will find yourself reading works published by small and independent presses. The major presses, those big New York publishers, the kind you see in movies with

editors who have improbably large discretionary funds, who give their writers absurdly large advances, they don't really want fiction that pushes envelopes. What they want is what has already proven to work. That which is popular and, most importantly, sells. They want fiction that has had all its sharp edges smoothed down so it will appeal to the most and widest range of people possible. They want their Horror to be relatively safe, relatively conservative, even if the stories themselves are about ugly brutal things. They don't want challenging.

But, in my opinion, the best Horror, the best fiction written through the lens of horror, is about challenging. Words like strange and weird aren't category names: they are descriptors. Horror fiction needs to talk about bizarre things, consider the unconsidered, and think through the unthinkable. And the best Horror fiction is about exploring. About looking into our terrors and anxieties and learning where they're from and what they mean. It means investigating the premise of otherworldly and extrapolating from it what its existence means to us and for us, and doing so in a way that's pretty to some, ugly to others, and grotesque to most. This is why good fiction written through the lens of horror is not universally loved or understood. It's challenging in a way that few readers are able to rise to meet. It's fiction that wouldn't survive in the light of a New York Publisher. It would wither and die. It needs to stay relegated to the shadows. Like fungus, that's the only place it can really grow.

I hear you, though. "What about [my favourite author]? They work in the big leagues. They are daring, are experimental. Both scares me and makes me think. What about [my favourite author]?" Your favourite author is the exception. Sure. Why not? Like what you want to like. But I think your favourite author is writing those big-league novels (and, let's face it, they're writing novels) that fall squarely in the genre of Horror. They are using Horror tropes and bolting them on other types of stories, transforming them into Horror. They may have found a new twist in the way they do it, they maybe have bolted Horror onto a compelling thriller, but what these stories don't do is explore Horror. Instead, they use Horror to explore other things. The truth is they don't need Horror to tell their stories. The Horror is a means to an end. It's a tool in the author's toolbox.

But what do I know, right? I've written horror stories for a few years, and I've read Horror stories for a few years longer than that, but I probably know just as little about Horror as anybody else. There are scholarly takes and philosophical takes and psychological takes. There are definitions that put it in context with all fiction that's come before, and others that put it in context with all history that's come before. There are as many definitions of Horror as there are stars in the sky. This is just the way I see Horror. Maybe you see it differently. I mean, I hope you see it differently, because I suspect that's what keeps a genre vibrant: the fact it's never just one thing.

GREY'S GROTESQUERIES

by Orrin Grey

KICKING OPEN DOORS TO LIGHT AND SHADOW:
THE CRESTWOOD HOUSE MONSTER BOOKS

Crestwood House Monster Series

I N HIS INTRODUCTION to the second volume of Mike Mignola, Christopher Golden, Ben Stenbeck, and Dave Stewart's wonderful gothic comic series *Baltimore*, no less a horror luminary than Joe R. Lansdale describes the original Universal monster movies, "with their wonderfully gothic sets and shifty-eyed peasants and shambling monsters and fluttering bats."

The comic, he continues, "goes where your mind went when you saw those films as a kid, goes where the film didn't, but you think it did, because at that age your mind is fresh and open and full of light and shadow, all of it moving about in savage flickers, having not yet settled and found its civilized position."

I didn't see the Universal movies that he's describing when I was a kid. I arrived late to the Universal monsters, to Hammer's gothic chillers, and all of their ilk. Born in 1981, I came into the world too late to be a true Monster Kid.

By the time I was watching television, schlock pictures like Squirm and The Food of the Gods had edged out the Shock Theater package of classic Universal flicks that provided a staple for horror hosts in the late '50s and into the '60s.

In their place, I had the Crestwood House monster books. Anyone of my age and proclivities knows the books well; if not by that name, then by a simple description — orange board books with distinctive fonts and a bat-shaped logo.

Each one of them focused on a monster or a monster movie. There were books for Universal greats like

Dracula, *Frankenstein*, the *Creature from the Black Lagoon*, and also *King Kong*, *Godzilla*, *The Blob*, *The Deadly Mantis*, and so on.

There were actually two series; the better-known orange books, which covered some of the bigger names, and a second series, retitled "Movie Monsters," with purple covers and an orange font that looked like a high school letter jacket. This second series dealt with lesser-known films like *The Mole People*, *Werewolf of London*, *House of Fear*, and sequels including *Bride of Frankenstein*, *Dracula's Daughter*, and *Revenge of the Creature*.

When I was very young, my school library had plenty of both. They are the first books I can really remember reading. The text inside, often by Julian Clare May writing as Ian Thorne, retold the stories of the movies, sure, but it also placed them in context. The *Dracula* one talked about Bela Lugosi and Bram Stoker's novel and other various cinematic adaptations of the Count. Ditto all the others.

I think that's important. I think it helped to establish in me a real curiosity for seeing the connections between movies and text, movies and one-another.

The writing was only the beginning, though. What *really* drew me to these books, kept me coming back time and time again, why I still remember them fondly to this day, was the pictures.

The Crestwood House monster books were illustrated throughout with enchanting and atmospheric black-and-white stills from the movies themselves. Movies that I had never seen. That I couldn't even *imagine* except insofar as those pictures provided a doorway through which I could peer at a world alive with "light and shadow, all of it moving about in savage flickers."

I didn't just look at those film stills — I *pored* over them. I fell into them and a part of me has never crawled back out. Some of my earliest storytelling came in the form of looking at those strange, staged, black-and-white photographs and trying to imagine the movie that they must have belonged to.

"For everything you see with your eyes at that age," Lansdale says of the Universal movies, "your mind's eye sees a hundred times more." If that's true of the films you actually *watch*, how much truer must it be of the ones that you cannot watch, but only long for, unearthing them piece-by-piece from pictures in library books, like an archaeologist conjuring dinosaurs from the imprints of old bones?

There was a thing that we all did when I was a kid, I don't have a name for it — I'm not sure if it's something people still do, in this age of streaming content and everything on-demand — but we would tell each other the movies we had watched, as best we remembered them, on the playground the next day, or as we stayed up far too late at sleepovers.

Of course, we watched movies, too, whenever our parents would allow us to rent them or go to the theater. Some of us could see R-rated movies, others could not. But

none of us could ever watch nearly as many as we wanted to.

So, to bridge the gap, we told what we knew, and embellished what we didn't. The films took on a life of their own, outside the confines of the theater or our VCRs. In telling one-another about them, we turned them into a mythology, inventing rules that the films themselves were never so clear about — this same tendency was later repurposed and transformed into one of the great horror franchises of *my* time, the *Scream* series.

What we were doing when we told each other about the movies that we had seen, or only *wanted* to see, was what I was doing when I looked

at those Crestwood House books as a kid and imagined the movies that they must have been describing. It's what I'm doing every time I sit down to write a story. Lansdale has a phrase to describe it — because of course he does — and he puts it better than I ever could — because, again, of course:

"Isn't that the job of all great art," he asks, "to kick open doors to light and shadow and let us view something that otherwise we might not see?"

He thinks it is, and so do I. And without those Crestwood House books to first force that door open a crack, I might never have gotten here.

FICTION

KRAZY KRAX

by Naben Ruthnum

SHE WAS TAKING the children, and was welcome to them. But she hadn't asked me first.

They were hers and I did not like them. And even after three years of determined pretending, they never even attempted to believe in my love, and were not grateful for my tolerance. Their names were Mark, who was 8, and Grosvenor, 11. Mark I could perhaps have liked, someday, when he was quieter. Grosvenor I never would have been able to tolerate. His name was Grosvenor, which was unacceptable, even if it was 'a family name,' as my wife told everyone she had a chance to introduce him to.

She had packed thoroughly for their departure. They managed to wake and head downstairs in near-silence, but I had not fallen asleep. I haven't slept through the night for a few months now, and on that night, I had reason to stay alert. It's another example of the consideration that I had always extended to her and the boys that I didn't let them know I could hear everything: the suitcases being hauled up from the basement, the boys shuffling and zipping. If she had asked, if she had consulted me, I would have helped her pack and even driven her, if I was sure she was ready to go.

I listened to their last moments together in the home from the top of the staircase, crouching behind the newel like a child spying on an adult party. The boys were almost sweet in their treachery, whispering and steering each other, as quiet as they had ever been. Grosvenor only spoke aloud once, to remind my wife of the roll of money — my money — kept in the spice cupboard cinnamon tin.

I waited until they had all of their bags in the car, until they'd made their last trip to the garage and it was just her, having a last look around the living room, investing her moment alone with significance. Then I came down. Unlike her, unlike the boys, I had learned to move quietly. I knew to walk on the outer edge of the stairs, where the carpet was thickest and there were no creaks to be triggered. I knew to skirt the walls when I reached the floor, to get between her and the door, to let the surprise come then.

AFTERWARDS, I went to the garage, pulling her behind me. The boys were waiting in the car. Grosvenor didn't even look up from the phone that his mother had insisted he was old enough to have. Mark looked at me and said "Mommy," and I said "No." When I came back in, I showered and slept for a long time, aiming to miss the highest heat of the afternoon.

Our little home in the woods near Grimsby, close to Niagara Falls, had everything I needed and lacked everything that she eventually insisted was crucial to her happiness, including air conditioning. The woods that she never made use of had all the shade and coolness she could have wanted, but she and the boys only moved between house and car.

I walked around the house with a cup of coffee. The new space that had been cleared by the absence of this family was immense, and I had to stand at the top of the staircase once again, this time erect and staring down into the tidiness of the living room for almost a full minute, to confirm that no furniture was gone.

I looked into the bedroom the boys had shared. They had packed their clothing and their toys, but left their collections. Each boy had placed his collection on his bed — surely Grosvenor's idea of a hurtful gesture. Mark always wanted to please Grosvenor or his mother, or he and I would have gotten along quite well.

I sat down on Mark's bed and picked up the stamp album. It had been mine, ages ago. I'd given him my childhood collection as a start on his, signed him up to a subscription club so he would have the thrill of receiving mail twice a month, and talked him through the history of philately.

"Why does it matter?" he'd asked, when I'd first given him the album and told him how long I'd spent with it when I was a boy.

"It doesn't," I said. "That's part of the point." He nodded as though he understood. We decided he would focus on collecting animal stamps.

Grosvenor's collection was in an album and a Keds shoebox. It was currency, and from the canny greed he'd displayed in directing his mother to the cinnamon tin, I was impressed that his dislike for me exceeded his desire to hold on to cash. We'd started Grosvenor off at a flea market here in Grimsby, late on a Sunday afternoon. A defeated vendor whose table was still full, and whose goods and person reeked of decades of cigarettes, allowed me to buy a starter collection of foreign notes — "Some of these are darn close to pre-WW1," he'd said, as he tried to bargain me up — for almost nothing. The price was so low that I took pity and bought a teapot from the man at sticker price. We never used it.

The latest addition to Grosvenor's collection was something I picked up in a pawnshop just across the border, in a small New York town off the track of regular Falls tourism. I opened the shoebox, expecting to see the prize on top, but saw only the mess of British, Samoan, Belgian, and other notes that he had never bothered to organize, despite the mylar sleeves I'd bought for him.

I was looking for a teller's envelope. It had been in the glass case at this pawn shop, and when I'd asked about it, the small and bored old woman who owned the place showed me the contents, pulling the small wad out with tweezers. Twenty crisp American one-dollar-bills from 1961, straight from the bank, uncreased. They were hers, the woman explained, an envelope she'd gotten before Christmas or a trip to the city back then. She couldn't remember whether the money had been intended to be presents for nephews or tips for bellhops, but she had misplaced it on a shelf of encyclopedias for sixty years, and now wanted five times face value. We bargained and I emerged with the envelope. When I reached home, I presented it to Grosvenor, hidden between the leaves of a book. He hated books, and I wanted to see him disappointed and surly, then ashamed of his attitude when he found his real gift. But when I gave it to him, on the porch swing where he was drinking his third cola of the day, the surly expression stayed in place even when he found the envelope and pulled out its contents, ignoring my hiss and admonishment to be delicate. "Thanks," he said. My wife witnessed all of this, and when I asked her to speak to him afterwards, she asked me exactly how much gratitude I needed from her children or herself. It would be useful to have a chart, she said.

The envelope wasn't in the shoebox. This began to make sense to me. The children thought they were heading across the border, so Grosvenor would have taken the money that he could use, while leaving the collection to insult me.

I walked out to the garage to reclaim the bills. I didn't know exactly why I wanted them, other than that I'd paid for them and he never appreciated them. Grosvenor was in the front passenger seat, wearing a light jacket which used to be blue. My wife always made the kids bring their jackets on outings, even in the summer. The teller's envelope was in Grosvenor's breast pocket, again hidden in a book. A comic book, this time. One of mine.

Sgt. Fury and His Howling Commandos. Issue 16, from March 1965. It had little market value, but had been with me for decades. I bought it at a gas station in Halifax sometime in the summer of 1965. This gas station held on to old issues of comics when the new ones came out, keeping them in a wooden crate that once held brake shoes. The crate fit the books well, let you flip through them easily, but issues touched the greasy concrete between the slats, and almost every book recovered had a quarter-inch oil stain at the bottom, soaked into every page. But they were five cents instead of twelve, and that's how I began the collection that now filled the third bedroom of my home.

I would have slapped Grosvenor if he could feel it. The comic was folded and stained, but its pages had kept the teller's envelope clean. I went inside, knowing I would have to destroy the issue, even if I wouldn't be around long enough to replace it. I couldn't let it survive me in this compromised condition, with this damage that had nothing to do with memories. But before I destroyed the book, I would read it again. I would honour it.

Aside from the tacky wetness, Grosvenor or Mark had vandalized the inner front cover of Sgt. Fury 16. It was one of those full-page ads for EXCLUSIVE FUN PRODUCTS BY MAIL that were ubiquitous in the comics of that era. Among those fun products were Pepper Gum, a Trick Baseball, a Prankster Whistle, Krazy Krax, a Silver Skull Ring, X-Ray-Spex.

The Silver Skull Ring had been circled in blue ballpoint pen. So had the Krazy Krax, which appeared to be a plastic film that could be placed over a window or television to make it appear broken.

I stopped reading the issue when I arrived at another envelope, stuck between pages 9 and 10. It was

addressed to ELLBAR DIST. Dept G.K. 12, Niagara Falls, N.Y., in Grosvenor's inept handwriting. This was the address from the bottom corner of the Fun Products ad. I checked the stock of dollar bills in the teller's envelope and found that it was four dollars short. This was perhaps the first time that Grosvenor ever gave me a genuine laugh.

I didn't have a plan for the bodies, because I hadn't understood that my wife was leaving until I found her own packed suitcases next to the basement deep-freeze, on the final morning of her last night. I had no visitors, but there would be questions, eventually. I was at peace with that, choosing to enjoy what undisturbed time I had left. There didn't need to be an escape. There didn't need to be a future. I imagined gracefully joining my hands for the cuffs, and explaining exactly where I'd buried them all to a policeman who remained faceless but who grudgingly admired my coolness. But it was more likely that I would get a phone call from my wife's mother to alert me that my time alone would soon be interrupted forever, and that would be when I'd draw a map to her and the boys, then lose myself in the woods with a jar of the correct pills.

Grosvenor's first package arrived two days after he was supposed to have left. Wrapped in more tape than necessary, with a small typed label, it was hardly larger than a pack of cigarettes. I threw out two flyers, opened a book I'd ordered from the UK and would never have the chance to read, a prospect that made me more immediately sad than any of my vaguer ruminations on an exit, and then started to open Grosvenor's box with a steak knife.

Packed in balls of cotton, it was the Silver Skull Ring that he had circled in the ad. With red glass ruby eyes, a square backing, and a fit that would have been too small even for my pinky but too large even for Grosvenor's thumbs, the skull was bright, and silver only in colour. It was undeniably cheap, and just as undeniably in perfect condition, as though mine were the first hands to touch it since 1965.

I hadn't been able to throw out Sgt. Fury 16, perhaps because I hadn't finished rereading it. I went back to the boys' bedroom, where it rested on the small desk. The price of the skull ring, which actually did fit on my pinky, if tightly, was $1.00. The coupon demanded a further fifteen cents for shipping. The teller's envelope had been missing four dollar bills: Grosvenor must have mailed an order and two bills before his departure as a testing salvo, but he sent it too late. The addressed envelope currently resting on Mark's bed would contain the other two dollars and

EXCLUSIVE FUN PRODUCTS BY MAIL

KRAZY KRAX

Just place this over the T.V. screen or the front window. Watch the fun begin. It looks like the glass is broken. No. 1004 .... .60

JUMPING CANDY BOX
Looks like a box of candy. When your friend goes to help himself he'll get the surprise of his life. No. 2015 ... Only .75

WHOOPS
Looks like someone lost their lunch. Place it on the floor and wait for your first unsuspecting victim to walk in—ugh. Better catch him before he faints. No. 9016 .... Only .75

TRICK BASEBALL
It bounces cockeyed, it curves, it dips, it's impossible to catch. It's sure to set all the kids on the block chasing after it. There's a barrel of fun in every bounce of this amazing baseball.
No. 4020 _____ 50¢

PRANKSTER WHISTLE
Greatest gag in years. Just place inside any tail-pipe and watch the fun. As soon as he starts the car it will sound as if the whole motor fell out. It's a panic, but completely harmless.
No. 7021 _____ 75¢

Loud Nose Blower
Blow your nose and it will sound like the roof caved in. Fits right in your handkerchief out of sight.
No. 6018..only 20¢

PEPPER GUM
Hi Pal, have a piece of gum. Once he starts chewing you better have a glass of water ready. Completely harmless but a million laughs. No. 5008... .25

JIU-JITSU

This is one of the most popular books on the art of self defense. Now you needn't back away from anyone. Many illustrations show you how to defend yourself from bullies. We also include "FREE" a book on strong man stunts. No. 4003....... Only $1.00

SQUIRT SEAT

Its all wet. Place it under the toilet seat. Can't you picture the expression on your victims face when he sits down? No. 6012 .... .75

WHOOPEE CUSHION
Place this under any cushion. Gives out a loud Bronx Cheer. Very embarrising but loads of laughs. No. 8010
Only .50

JOY BUZZER
Shake hands and watch your friend jump 6 feet high. Completely harmless. No. 7005 .... .50

SURPRISE PACKAGE
If you are willing to take a chance, we guarantee you more than your moneys worth, filled with surprises. No. 8002.. .50

SCREWY FEET
These magnetic feet will stick to anything. Paste them to the walls and ceiling. 12 to a set. Looks like the invisible man just walked through the wall. No. 2007 $1.00

SILVER SKULL RING
Heavy Mexican silver ring with the raised face of skull and inlayed red ruby eyes. Feels good and looks real impressive. Adds heft to your hands.
No. 3019 _____ $1.00

X-RAY-SPEX

A wonderful illusion to fool your buddies.
Put them on, now is that really his skull you see inside his head? Prove to him you can see through anything. No. 7014 .... $1.00

BIKE SPEEDOMETER
Now you can tell how fast you are going. Registers speeds up to 50 miles per hour. New built-in compass also shows in what direction you are travelling. Fits any bicycle. Attaches in seconds.
No. 3017 only 75¢

SILENT DOG WHISTLE

This whistle can not be heard by any human, but your pet will hear it blocks away. Everyone will be amazed when he comes running as soon as he hears his own private whistle. No. 1009 Only $1.00

FLY IN ICE
A plastic ice cube that looks like the real thing, only with a fly inside. Just place this in someones drink when he isn't looking—ugh. No. 3011
Only .45

ELLBARR DIST. DEPT. GK 11 NIAGARA FALLS, N.Y.
RUSH ME THE ITEMS LISTED BELOW. If I am not 100% delighted, I may return any part of my purchase after the 10 day free trial for full refund.

ITEM No.	NAME OF ITEM	HOW MANY	TOTAL PRICE

☐ I enclose ...... plus 15c postage and shipping in cash, cheque or money order.

NAME ....
ADDRESS ....

a poorly handwritten order for Krazy Krax, the other item that the boy had coveted.

I stared at the ring on my finger. It was beginning to itch and irritate, as cheap metals will, so I pulled it off. Surely it was almost as worthless now as it had been back then, but it was miraculously new.

I checked again for stains, traces, droplets on the envelope Grosvenor had addressed and kept close to his heart on the night he was meant to leave here. I stared at the stamps, which I hadn't looked at properly before. Two Canadian 5¢ stamps, uncancelled, marine blue, with the queen's head in profile. I'd put them in the stamp album myself in 1962, or perhaps 1963.

I had to wait until night before I drove into town to slip the envelope into a mailbox. We only had the one car, and I hadn't been able to clean the front seat well enough. I came home with a pizza and slept on the couch with my new ring on.

I thought the package arrived too quickly, but then realized that a 2-day response was possible. Ellbarr Distribution was in another country, but only a forty-minute drive away. This time the box was flat and long, the tape not just excessive, but mummifying. When I did get it open, a pristine branded package fell out: Krazy Krax, with a Hank Ketcham style cartoon of a harried mother exclaiming Oh Dear! More Expense! in front of a television with what appeared to be a shattered screen. Two children leered behind her. I concentrated carefully on this part of the drawing. If my wife had anticipated all of this, if she had engineered it, her precise idea of a joke, of a clue that I would be too stupid to understand, would be to draw these children as Mark and Grosvenor.

There was no resemblance.

I spent more time with Sgt. Fury that evening, after unpacking the Krazy Krax item and adhering it to the flat-screen in the living room. It covered a bit less than half of the surface. I could order Screwy Feet, magnetic feet that would stick to anything. A Fly In Ice. A Loud Nose Blower. A Squirt Seat. A Jiu Jitsu manual.

A Surprise Package. If you are willing to take a chance, we guarantee you more than your moneys worth, filled with surprises. No. 8002... .50¢. That would be the one that she would want me to order, that Grosvenor, who was so much more imaginative than I had thought, would have been attracted to next. I wouldn't do it.

I looked at the address again, memorizing it before I walked out to the car. Dept G.K. 12, Niagara Falls, N.Y. No street name, which implied that Ellbarr Distribution was so vast, so knowable, that the post office in 1962 hadn't needed the street, let alone the zip codes that wouldn't come into existence until the next year.

The passenger seat looked innocuous enough when I put an overnight bag on it. But I hadn't realized that some of Grosvenor's spray, quite a bit of it, must have gotten onto the driver's seat as well. My back had warmed it up, made it liquid again. I could feel it absorbing into my t-shirt, forcing me to sit absolutely straight, to leave no crack open to vision as I approached the border. The guard only asked me one question.

"Overnighting at the Ramada to get a jump on antiquing tomorrow," I said. He waved me through while I was still speaking. I was old, so he believed me.

I was lost quite soon. I drove through the mill district, looking at dark looming buildings, at abandoned plants, at lofts converted into overnight tourist rentals. I was quite stuck to my seat with Grosvenor's moisture, now. I remembered that he had dropped his phone when I put the knife into his brother, that he had let it go and reached for me before I reached for him. I picked the phone out of the gap between the passenger seat and the centre console and used it to search for Ellbarr Distribution. Grosvenor's mother hadn't allowed him to put a password onto the phone.

It was on Highland Avenue. I drove straight there, using the phone's voice to navigate, ignoring traffic lights and my own sense of direction. It was after midnight but the warehouse, as huge as I'd imagined, glowed and clattered with life, the sound of loaders and conversation, of men filling orders, of order itself.

I parked and entered. Inside, it was dark, but the machines and conversation continued, and I could feel the workers moving around me, sometimes through me. None of them stopped when I spoke.

I had brought the rest of Grosvenor's dollars, and knew that it was his hand I felt on them, in my pocket, and his other small hand I felt on the wet back of my shirt, wanting his blood back. The other hands touched me soon, a small pair at my knees, and hers at my neck. I took the skull ring off to offer it to Grosvenor, but he had taken what he wanted and was gone. She stayed with me, her fingers stronger now than they ever were before. I think Mark took the ring, because my last memory is not of dropping it, but of her face somehow entering mine. My hands were empty by then, as they are still.

FICTION

WHITE NOISE IN A WHITE ROOM

by Steve Duffy

THE SCHOOLHOUSE stood apart from the rest of the village, at the top of a small rise on the road to Crossmaglen. Originally, it had been enclosed by a low wall with railings; now, steel shuttering ten feet high blocked it from the view of passers-by. Those few people who gained admittance through the solid steel gates found themselves in the old playground, still marked for five-a-side and handball but now a parking space for Army vehicles. Ahead of them was the schoolhouse, its high windows shuttered against the daylight, and against whatever else Armagh might launch at it.

Inside the building, the window-glass was painted over in regulation drab green. The former headmaster's room was lit by fluorescent strips; their light reflected wanly from the institutional brown gloss on the walls before it lost itself on the dusty parquet floor. Filing cabinets stood behind the large desk which confronted the guest directly on entering. The tableau reminded the visitor of courts-martial he had attended in his past life.

In the whole of the room there were only two splashes of vividness: the egg-and-bacon MCC tie of the man who sat before the desk in a cheap stacking chair, and the carmine-red folder placed squarely in the centre of the desktop.

From outside in the corridor came the sound of footsteps. The visitor rose as the door opened. "Captain — I'm sorry, Major now, I see. Congratulations."

"Hello, sir — very glad you could come. Much appreciated." The two men shook hands. "I hope the crossing was uneventful?"

"The ferry, you mean? Or the soft crossing at Dogans Bridge? Both entirely straightforward, I'm glad to say."

"That's a relief. Tell me, did you like Staniforth? He's my driver — one of the few people I can tolerate being driven by. Now then, let's see." The major settled himself in the chair behind the desk. "Have they given you a cup of tea and a biscuit? Ah, they have, good. Smoke?" He pushed a tinfoil ashtray towards his visitor

The visitor shook his head. "No, thanks all the same." He looked around the room. "So this is your operation now?"

"Since my promotion in '74, yes sir. And how about you? Enjoying retirement and so forth? Do you miss your old place up in the Welsh wilds?"

"Since Merlyn Rees mothballed us? Not really. I still do the odd bit of civvy work at the barracks in Ashford, you know, visiting lecturer for the new intake. This — " he patted the canvas holdall at the side of his chair — "has been at the back of the wardrobe for quite a few years now."

"It's very much their loss." The major paused. "I'd heard you hadn't been well?"

"Nothing to write home about," the visitor said levelly. "People make a lot of these things. Unnecessarily, I think. One arrives at a certain equilibrium."

"I mean, obviously, I wouldn't have involved you, if the situation hadn't been..." The major shook his head. "Unusual."

"Whatever help I can give," the visitor said. "Perhaps if you let me have a look?" He gestured towards the red file on the desk. "I take it this is Chummy?"

"Yes, sir." The major pushed the file across to his visitor. He took from his pocket a packet of cigarettes, and placed them in the same central spot on the desk that the file had previously occupied, as if it was somehow important in the scheme of things. "You'll notice there isn't a name."

"Yes, so I see." The visitor folded the cover of the file back, began to read.

"That's not just because he isn't talking. Though he isn't, you know. We've taken his prints, gone through his belongings, even asked Special Branch to turn over his digs. Absolutely nothing. The name he was renting under is not a name that appears in any register of births."

"Puts us at something of a social disadvantage," remarked the visitor. His tone was easy, yet the major took it as an invitation to silence. Accordingly, he waited the fifteen minutes or so it took his visitor to read all the way through the file. When he closed it and replaced it on the desk, the officer stubbed out his JPS in the exact centre of the ashtray and took up more or less where he had left off.

"As things stand, sir, that file represents the only bit of paperwork on Chummy in the system. And I mean in any system: he's not on the electoral register; he hasn't got a jacket with the local police; he doesn't own a home, pays cash on the nail for a rented room; and most pertinently of all, he turns up nowhere in regular intel. When he came on the Army's radar, he was pushed all the way up the line to us immediately. He didn't have time to accumulate anything in the way of bumf."

"I see. Well, on the one hand it's a little hard to see how one might proceed with the case. But on the other, I suppose the circumstances grant you a certain latitude, don't they?"

"Well, there is that, sir." The major grinned ruefully. "It's a relief to know there won't be any knocks on the door from the civil rights brigade, or the local padre wanting to give him Holy Communion."

The visitor was studying him narrowly, in a way that some people might have found disconcerting. "But that's your only relief in the matter, really. I mean, reading through the file, this is a terrible thing that he did."

The major grimaced, raised his hands vaguely, folded them back on his desk. "It is. Thank God we made our move before the civilian authorities got wind of it, that's all. Our men were in and out of there in an evening: we got our man, brought him back across the border and the Gardai knew nothing about it till the morning after, when somebody stumbled on the cave.

"By then the legend was already in place, to the effect that what was found in there were the bodies of suspected informers, people who'd been kidnapped, subjected to kangaroo courts, then been the victims of summary Republican justice. Naturally, the Provos denied it, and naturally, people will believe whatever they're predisposed to believe. Already, events have moved on. Except here, at the schoolhouse."

He sighed. "Basically, we're complicit in the covering up of half a dozen deaths, and we haven't even got the one thing that would make that remotely acceptable in the bigger scheme of events."

"You haven't got the intel."

"Exactly, sir."

The visitor regarded him as closely and as non-judgementally as he had examined the red folder. "Very well. Let's take this business in the file about how he came into your hands."

"Yes sir: well, that was curious from the very beginning. We had a tip-off about him from one of our best and most trusted sources inside the Provisional IRA. Night-time flits across the border to a site on a beach in County Louth, vague talk of a cave in the cliffs, people disappearing. All very suggestive. But what was most interesting was the commentary on all of this, so to speak, from our deep source. So far as we could make out, the Provos were washing their hands of him. He wasn't just being cut loose, he was being offered to us quite deliberately, as if they wanted rid of him."

The visitor nodded. "Normally, of course, when the Provisionals want rid of somebody..."

"He ends up face down in a ditch, quite. So the fact that this hadn't happened — that they were willing in fact to betray him to the enemy — was the first indication that all wasn't what it seemed.

"Our first thought was that this was a plant: that he was being handed over to us stuffed to the gills with phoney intel, which he'd deliver up to us with a becoming show of reluctance. We were entirely prepared for that. We felt ourselves perfectly able to sift through the nonsense and get to the facts of the matter; we prided ourselves on it, you might say. But then we took him — ambush at the scene of the crime, into the back of a van with a bag over his head, spirited seamlessly out of the world in the course of a night's work — and we found..." He tailed off.

"You found him uncommunicative," the visitor suggested.

"For which we were signally unprepared."

"The level of his uncommunicativeness — "

"The level and the nature of it. Unlike anything I'd ever ... we'd ever encountered. There wasn't anybody who'd come across anything quite like it. Which was why, eventually, I came to think of you. As my mentor, you might say."

"Charmed." The two men shared a weary smile.

"I always remember something you said, on that very first course I attended. That there was a crack in everybody's armour, that all you had to do was turn him around and around till you caught sight of it. Good advice, I thought. It's certainly worked up till now."

"Regarding Chummy, then. I take it all the usual procedures were followed?"

"Well, I don't need to tell you, do I, sir? The squad who picked him up followed RA1 to the letter, working straight from the trade textbook. By the time he was handed over to us he ought to have been ready for processing. So we started right in on the five techniques." He counted them off on his fingers.

"Hooding: more or less continuous, and he seems fine with it. White noise: ditto. Sleep deprivation: the bugger scarcely seems to sleep at all as it is. Postural: again, we could have him doing ballet poses on one leg and it wouldn't faze him. Dietary: he's been on bread and drain since he came in. He eats what we give him with no complaint, and it has no effect."

"So you moved to the specialized procedures."

The major nodded. "Yes. I'll be honest, we don't operate under much scrutiny here. Water treatment, jump-leads, you name it. After a spell with us, Castlereagh probably feels like the Europa Hotel. We have been patient and creative in our techniques. You'd have been proud of us." The visitor raised an eyebrow.

"And the sum total of our efforts so far? He hasn't even opened his mouth to confirm the name he was using when he was snatched. Nothing."

"I see," said the visitor. "So that's the reason you brought me over, is it?"

"Yes and no. It's for my own peace of mind as much as anything, by this time. You see what he's done. Terrible things. Terrible. Like nothing we've ever seen, even over here."

"Like nothing I've ever seen anywhere."

"Quite, sir. And that's saying a lot, given your experience."

"And we believe them, do we? Even the rumours, these stories from the informers?"

"Where they're checkable, they have indeed checked out, sir. As the evidence in the cave confirms."

The visitor grimaced. "And of course, whatever happens, you can't just produce him now, can you?"

"Of course not." The major took another cigarette from the packet, tapped it nervously on the desk. "No, we bypassed the chance of a judicial outcome when we vanished him. He'll never face trial. We thought it would be worth it if he was high up in the Provisional structure, in terms of the intel we might glean. And now, we're stuck with him."

"And he's no good to anyone."

"Up to a point. Though it would be good to know. Necessary, in fact, to know that it was him. That all of it was down to him and him alone. I mean, it's gone beyond intel gathering now. But without a confession nobody's the wiser."

The major lit his cigarette, and the visitor noticed a slight tremor in the hand that applied the lighter. "I keep coming back to the Provos. To the reason they effectively handed him over to us. I've come to the conclusion they were like us: they were afraid of him. Because we are afraid of him, very much so."

The words hung in the stuffy air between them. The visitor said nothing, but continued to watch the major as he drew on his cigarette. After a while, the major said: "Not a thing to be particularly proud of, is it?"

"Pride shouldn't really come into it," said the visitor instantly. "It's always important for an inquisitor to be completely honest with himself when assessing his reactions in the interrogation process. There is no shame in honesty."

"I know, sir," the major said. "Still: there it is. Simply by being there — by sitting in a crate and not lifting a finger — he's beating us. And I feel... I feel it's important that he not beat us. After what he's done."

The visitor considered this for a minute. Then he said: "You'd like me to have a go at him."

"Yes, sir. Yes, I would. I realise this is totally irregular, that you're retired, a civilian. I could end up on a hell of a fizzer if anybody found out about it. But this is the schoolhouse: nobody will ever find out what goes on in here. Nobody cares to know."

The visitor considered this. "If the Provos have disowned him, if he was never really working for them, then anything he gives you will hardly be relevant in the military sense."

"Doesn't matter, sir. At this stage, it really doesn't matter. I just want to hear from his own lips who he is and what he did — why, too, if you can possibly get that out of him — and then I just want to be rid of him." The visitor looked up sharply. "One way or the other," the major added.

The visitor nodded. "Over and above all this, you realise that there's a reason I was invited to retire? You know that a medical tribunal reviewed my work and decided I was to be cut loose? I don't expect the details ever came out, but you know that I had no choice in the matter? That had I not retired, I would have been removed? On psychiatric grounds?"

The major was already shaking his head. "Quite aware of that, sir. I still regard you as the best. There is literally nobody else I would trust in the matter.

Nobody whatsoever. My show; my rules."

The visitor allowed himself a smile. "You're too kind, major. After such a ringing endorsement, I only hope I don't let you down. Very well, then. I shall see what I can do. This need never be mentioned outside this room?"

"No, sir, absolutely not."

"I shall want to see him alone, I think. No guards present. What's his current status?"

"At the moment, lights out, shackles, hooded. To be honest, that's as much to do with our own delicate sensibilities as anything. Nobody wants to be in there with him. I've spent hours in there, we all have, and it's a profoundly disturbing experience. He was fed at 0400 hours, and it's now — " he consulted his watch — "nearly midday. I think we might forego lunch."

The visitor rose from his chair, stretched, and cracked his knuckles. The noise seemed very loud in the stillness of the schoolroom. "Righto," he said, and bent to pick up his holdall. "Take me to Chummy, then."

The major breathed deeply for a second or two, then rose in his turn.

The two men walked along the ill-lit corridor to a door at the farther end, which was stencilled in white paint with the words ABSOLUTE SILENCE. Inside the large bare assembly hall stood what looked like a rectangular shipping container, made of steel and painted military grey. In the middle of the container's long side there was a padlocked door, next to which Staniforth and a corporal were sitting on two more of the plastic stacking chairs. The visitor assumed they had belonged in the schoolroom, back in the day. Hanging from the back of the corporal's chair was a Sterling Mk.4 submachine gun.

They scrambled to attention as the major approached, but he waved them back down. "Stand easy, you two," he said quietly. "Our guest is going to have a word with Chummy. I want you to listen very carefully, and if you hear anything untoward,

anything, I want you in there right away, firearms at the ready, understand? Do not wait to be invited."

"What's the disposition of the seating?" asked the visitor.

"He'll be on the left as you enter, sir," the guard said, "and your seat will be on the right."

"Bear that in mind if you do feel the need to join us," the visitor said. "And if I do give the signal, don't stand on ceremony. Well." He smiled at each man in turn. "Are we ready, then?"

The two men looked at the major, who nodded. The guard turned a key in the padlock and stood aside from the door. The visitor nodded in thanks and went in. The men heard a click and a buzz as the fluorescent light came on inside the container, saw flat light spilling from the doorway for a moment before the door was quietly and firmly closed.

"ARE YOU READY to come out, sir?"

Staniforth's voice reached him as if from a long way away. Standing there in the gloom, his ears had been filled with the sound of waves on pebbles, or it might have been one of his own tape recordings of white noise. At high volume it could break a man; played softly, it had often helped him fall asleep.

"Yes; yes, I'll be with you now." When he turned towards the mouth of the cave, Staniforth was silhouetted there, with the grey shingle beach and the waves behind him.

"We've got plenty of time, sir. The ferry doesn't sail till eight."

"Righto." He picked his way around the saltwater pools and clumps of seaweed. Staniforth watched him solicitously.

"It's been cleaned up, of course, sir," he said. "Off bounds as far as the authorities can make it, though to be honest, sir, I don't think anybody wants to come here anyway."

"No, I should think not," said the visitor. He emerged into the drab afternoon, the susurrus of the waves still churning through his head. "Have you by any chance got a smoke, sergeant?"

"Certainly, sir." Staniforth produced a packet of Bensons, held his lighter for the visitor.

"I don't, normally," he said, turning the cigarette this way and that as if unsure how to hold it. "Still."

"Absolutely, sir," Staniforth said. "Mind if I join you, sir?"

"Please." The two men smoked in silence for a minute or two. Then the visitor asked, "Were you a member of the patrol that first entered the cave, sergeant?"

"I was, sir," Staniforth said. A spasm of disgust pulled at his face. "A nasty business, sir. Fucking horrible, actually, beg your pardon."

"I completely agree." The visitor was carefully not looking in Staniforth's direction. "I think I saw in the case file that one of the men is still on psychiatric leave."

"That's right, sir," Staniforth agreed. "Young Belkin." He paused, as if wondering how much he could, or should, say. "I did say to the lieutenant, sir, at the time. I mean, he's only on his first tour. The lieutenant, too," he added, scrupulously.

"Oh, it's no respecter of experience or of rank," the visitor said. "I've been through a mandatory evaluation myself, you know. Quite a thorough one, for all the good it did me." He flicked his cigarette butt on to the wet sand. "How long have you been out here, sergeant? In Erin's green valleys?"

"Four years this coming January, sir," he said. "I tell you, though, in all that time, I've never seen anything like what we found in there."

"I imagine not," said the visitor.

"Sir?" There was an earnest, hesitant quality in Staniforth's voice that made the other man turn and look at him. "Sir, me and the lads were just saying before — well, we wanted to thank you."

"Thank me? For what?"

"For what you did. For taking it out of the major's hands, sir."

"I see." The visitor threw his cigarette into the thin wash of the tide. "Well, I dare say you've all been ordered not to talk about that, no?"

" 'Course, sir. And you needn't have any worries on that score, sir, not at all. But between ourselves?" He paused, and again some strong emotion seemed to cramp the muscles in his face. "I don't think there was any other way around it, is all."

"It was hardly textbook." The visitor was watching Staniforth's face narrowly. "It wasn't a thing I have ever done before, not in all my years in the service. Looked at in that light, it was not only a failure, it was inexcusable. It was, in fact, the very sort of thing I was warned might happen. Why I was instructed to retire, several years ago. Why I ought not to have come back."

"But what was the alternative, sir?" Staniforth offered him another cigarette; with a slight hesitation he accepted. "What were we going to do with the bastard?"

"Not that." He gripped the hand that offered him the flame. "Never that."

"You say, that, sir, but what, then? The Provos didn't want him. The rozzers might think they want him, but they don't, not really, and we couldn't give him up if they did. Nobody wanted him, and we were stuck with him. And we couldn't get rid of him. And now, you've managed to get the job done at a stroke. Good show, sir."

"But of course we'll never learn the truth now, will we?"

"Suppose that doesn't matter, sir?"

"But the truth is supposed to matter. That's supposed to be our job, to uncover it. *Magna est veritas et praevalebit.*"

"That's a value judgement, sir. They're above my pay grade, those."

The older man drew deeply on his cigarette, exhaled the smoke as if it disgusted him. "I see," he said. "Very fair point." After a pause he went on:

"Let me tell you a story, Staniforth. A war story,

the ones we old soldiers bore you young fellers half to death with. Or I should say a post-war story.

"At the very beginning of my time in the service, I was part of the British Army's team in Nuremberg, for the trials of the Nazi war criminals. I saw them all, all those monsters you know from the newsreels and the history books. I saw Göring and Ribbentrop and Dönitz and Hess. I saw Ley, hanging in his cell; I saw Göring sprawled out on his bunk after swallowing his cyanide pill. I saw Rosenberg the Jew-baiter, the editor of *Der Stürmer*, the man who paved the road to the gas chambers, groaning in the latrines with a colossal dose of diarrhoea.

"These were all men who to a greater or lesser degree had committed unspeakable evil. And I looked at them in the dock, shabby downcast prisoners with buttons missing from their clothes and stubble on their chins, and I asked myself, 'Well then: is this the face of evil?' And you had to keep reminding yourself of what they'd done, because in the dock they looked... normal. Unexceptional. It's rather hard to believe in monsters when they ask for darning wool to mend their holey socks, or beg you for pile ointment or whatever. It was in a very real sense the beginning of my education.

"Now Nuremberg was in the American zone of occupation, but the trials were obviously a quadripartite arrangement. There were the Americans, the French, the British, and there were the Russians. Each nation had its own people at the court, and just as we represented the British Army, there were military teams from the other three allied countries. I got to know some of them pretty well: I socialized with several of the French junior officers, played chess with one of the Russians, their military liaison chap, when I had an evening spare. Anyway, there was one other man on the Soviet team I found quite striking: a reserved man, I didn't think he spoke any English, though I could never be sure how much of it he understood. I noticed that he didn't always use the headphones for translation in court, for instance.

"I became slightly obsessed by this man. For all sorts of reasons, my curiosity was engaged: by his manner, which was imperturbable; by his complete self-possession. Do you understand what I mean? He was, you'd say, an enigma. Over the weeks and months, I became preoccupied with him — I think I almost came to idolize him, in a way, though I hardly knew the first thing about him.

"There was a feeling abroad at that time, you see, that the Soviets were the bravest of the brave. We all had a pretty good idea of the scale of the battles on the Eastern front, the sacrifices they'd made, and, well, I looked at this chap and I seemed to see all the immense resolve of the Russian national character. The inner strength, the nobility, the determination to carry on no matter what. Silly, I know, but you must remember I was a young man in extraordinary times, and young men are prone to that sort of sentimental thinking.

"Well, it so happened that one evening in the January of 1946, this officer came into the watchroom when I was playing chess with my Russian colleague. He sat down and watched our game, and when it came to an end — I'd won, which didn't happen nearly as often as I'd have liked — I offered him the next round, out of politeness.

"He seemed not in the least surprised. He nodded, and sat at the table, and I switched to black, and... well, I won't burden you with the details, but he ground me down over the course of one of the longest hours you could imagine. He picked me off remorselessly, piece by piece. In the end there was nothing for it but to resign, which I did, and he smiled, just slightly, shook my hand and left the room. A firm handshake, correct, not overlong. I've often thought about it since.

"That was the end of the chess for the evening, but my curiosity about the other man was stoked even higher than it had been. I pressed my Russian colleague for details, just between the two of us. He looked at me for a long time, then suggested we go outside for a breath of air. Here, it was understood, we would not be overheard.

"It was snowing outside, and all the ruins — Nuremberg was smashed all to pieces still in that winter, great black heaps of rubble and charred timbers and the shells of buildings open to the sky — all the ruins were blanketed in white. All sounds were deadened; not a person moved on the streets.

"The Russian buried his chin deep in his fur collar, so that the steam of his breath hardly escaped, and this is what he said, just barely loud enough for me to hear:

" 'There is a monastery, not far from Moscow, near Lenin's dacha at his Gorki estate. It is a prison now, called Sukhanovka. Of all the prisons, it is the most feared. When a prisoner in one of our other facilities is threatened with Sukhanovka, he will confess on the spot, confess to anything, sign any declaration of guilt that is placed before him. Yezhov of the NKVD established it, Yezhov who was feared by all. Within a year he himself had been swallowed up by it. This is its power. Everything, everybody, it devours alike.

" 'You are taken there in a truck, by yourself. No other prisoners travel with you, and the guards are under instruction never to respond if you try to talk to them. This is how you arrive. How then do you leave? You do not leave. Nothing comes out of there: there are sixty-eight cells, cells of the monks, now cells of the prisoners, and nothing comes out of them. Nothing and no one. Not even a sound. Prisoners simply vanish; sometimes they scream, because they must, but their screams are instantly silenced. After a while they go insane and then they disappear, and in the space they leave behind there is only a terrible stillness.

" 'Your opponent at chess this evening: he was at Sukhanovka from the beginning. He was the most feared of its operatives. Stalin chose him personally to come here to Nuremberg, because he is certain that sooner or later our allies will come to their senses, these ridiculous trials will come to an end, and these prisoners, these fascists, they too will vanish. And this duty will be entrusted to my comrade, the man with whom you played your game of chess.'

"And there it was. He would say no more about it, not that evening, not ever again. And I think ever since that night, when I have looked at myself in the mirror at the end of a day's work, I have asked myself: who is it that you see? Whom do you most resemble today? The nondescript monsters of Nuremberg, or the quiet man of Sukhanovka? And as I stare at that reflection I wonder if what we see in the white room mightn't also be a mirror, of sorts. In a room filled with mirrors, I wonder what we'd really see? Might not anybody go mad in such a place as that, sergeant?"

Staniforth listened in silence, his face scrunched up a little with the strain of comprehension. For a while he said nothing, then, as if contradicting the visitor: "That one in the schoolhouse, though? We didn't drive him bonkers, sir. Quite the opposite, I'd say. And if you hadn't done what you did, sir, I honestly think he might have finished us all off in the end.

"I saw it with my own two eyes, sir. Men would go in with him, trained men, tough men, the toughest, and they'd come out no use for anything. Ruined, some of 'em. Finished. It wasn't natural. I can't find an explanation for that, sir. Are there just monsters, is that it? Like your Nazis, or that Russian bastard, or like Chummy? Do they come along once in a blue moon, sir? Real, honest-to-goodness monsters?" The sergeant's face was creased up in incomprehension and disgust.

"Am I an expert?" The other spoke so softly that it was hard to hear him above the noise of the waves sifting through the shingle.

"More of an expert than me, at any rate. More than any of us. That's why you were called in, wasn't it, sir?"

"No." Instantly. "I don't have any magical ability. I'm not St George fighting the dragons. I can't see what others don't. I was called in because... well, because of my historical track record in getting results from interrogations. A record, let me remind you, that has been called into question in the severest possible terms. Results, sergeant: not dead ends."

"Perhaps a dead end was the best thing for everybody, sir."

"Maybe. But you'll never know now, will you?"

"Don't care about that sir." The sergeant was dogmatic. "They whys and wherefores — I honestly don't give a toss."

"Don't you? It seems to be the only thing that matters to me. Why he came to do it, why such a thing came to be. That seems to me to be a necessary question, a question worth asking."

The sergeant considered this for a while. "But..." he began, then seemed to lose his way. After a moment or two he resumed: "What it is, sir, I'm happy with it all being a mystery. Not happy. Satisfied, whatever. Resigned to it. Like I said, it's above my pay grade." He seemed very anxious to convince the visitor. "You're better off leaving some things be, sir, if you ask me. If you look into the void for too long... well, you know how that one goes, sir, better than me, I'd say. There's such a thing as asking too many questions."

"Life asks us questions," said the other man. "That's what life does. I don't know, Staniforth. Perhaps where we go wrong is assuming that these questions always have an answer."

"Well, that's what I was saying, sir."

"Is it?" There was genuine surprise in his voice. "Is it really? Then perhaps we're just talking at cross purposes." The thought seemed to pain him.

The sergeant shook his head. "I think we're on the same hymn sheet really, sir. You know what I reckon? Sometimes, the hardest thing to do is to see what's right in front of you."

The other seemed hardly to hear him, staring out at the grey that met the grey at the indefinite cold horizon. "Anyhow," he said eventually, "I suppose we'd better be on our way."

The sergeant started to say something; then his face folded in on itself and he kept his mouth closed. In the end he simply nodded and saluted. The two men walked away from the cave mouth and towards the rotting wooden steps that led up to the parked car at the top of the bluffs.

THE LOUNGE OF the passenger ferry hosted a small group of determined drinkers: to call them "revellers" might be to overstate the case. The man with the canvas holdall sat on the opposite side of the room from them, writing in a notebook, with a cup of instant coffee untouched on the table in front of him. The liquid was sloshing gently in the moderate swell of the passage, and after a while he began to find this motion actively unpleasant. He got up and moved the coffee to the next table, then resumed his place.

The book was a school notebook. It might have come from a pile of such books in the schoolhouse on the Crossmaglen road. For the last hour he had been filling it with homework of a very particular kind, writing in his neat, tightly compacted script, barely pausing to search for the words. The current page began:

"In that cave I thought of the dakhmas of the Zoroastrians, the towers of silence. The temples of excarnation, where the bodies of the dead are pecked apart by birds so that demons might not rush into the corpses and pollute them.

"All around the edges of silence there lies madness. Just as matter begins to warp at the edge of a black hole, sanity begins to warp in the borderland of silence. In that cell I was morbidly conscious of the tinnitus that has plagued me in my advancing years, the sound of the blood rushing through my arteries that my doctor has warned me bodes no good. I heard the hum of electricity in the fluorescent tube, which might for all I know be the sound of the cloud of electrons flowing from filament to filament, ionizing the mercury vapour and coaxing light from it. I thought I might go mad. Perhaps if I had stayed in that room I might have heard the magnetic field of the earth, or the tectonic plates shifting a millimetre somewhere infinitely far beneath us. I might have heard the voice of God, or even worse, His critical and everlasting silence."

He picked up his pen and without bothering to reread what he had written, he went on:

"If I thought any of this made sense to anybody but the subject, it wouldn't be quite so bad. Of course, he knew. Chummy knew. It was the source of his strength, or at least the outward manifestation of it. It is why he remained invulnerable while the rest of us faltered, one by one. He was comfortable with it, if you like. He had accepted it.

"When the shot came I was so relieved to hear it. I thought the hammer might have fallen as if on fresh air, the primer might have exploded into a vacuum, the propellant might have puffed noiselessly from the barrel, the bullet struck its target and never made a single sound. I wondered whether that terrible vortex might have swallowed the shot entire, leaving no sign of its existence. It does not seem impossible to me that such a thing might happen, out beyond the event horizon. The Dionysiac architects, it is said, knew the secret of constructing chambers in which people could not hear their own screams."

For a while he considered what he'd written, then added another sentence: "Those places in which God is silent, while we babble." He closed the book, and then opened it again. Below the rest of the text he scribbled: "Burn this once you've read it."

Out on deck, the gangways were slick and treacherous. A fog had fallen on the Irish Sea since they had left Dun Laoghaire, and the ferry's speed had been reduced on the approach to Holyhead.

The man made his way to a place that was not overlooked by a lighted window, and stood at the rusted rail. He withdrew from his holdall a compact service revolver, hefted it as if to assess its weight. He held it out over the rail, high above the waves, let it dangle from his finger by the trigger guard, and hesitated a long moment before dropping it back into the bag. The ferry pushed on through the night, the sound of the engines baffled by the fog. After a while lights, red and white with an eerie afterglow, signalled the approach to South Stack and the terminal beyond, and he went back indoors.

On disembarking, the land seemed uncertain under his feet, as if it might suddenly begin to tilt and pitch like the deck of the ferry. Flashing a pasteboard card the size of a library ticket, the man slipped past the customs officials. Leaving the terminal building by a side door, he crossed the car park to his vehicle, a two-tone brown estate car drained of colour beneath the sickly sodium lights. Absentmindedly he removed the parking ticket from under the windscreen wiper, tore it to pieces, and got in.

The fog stayed with him through the drive across the flat scraped plains of Anglesey, and the crossing of the Menai strait, the waters invisible beneath the dark iron bulk of Telford's bridge. On the A55, headed for England and home, he found himself, almost unconsciously, taking the A5 exit then turning off past Bethesda. This was quarry country, bare rough rock crowding on either side of the narrow road, sharp friable layers of slate tipped precariously as if caught in the act of sliding down.

One more turn on to a minor road that nosed between the Snowdonia foothills, and then on to a track hewed between vertical cliff faces that fell away after a mile or two to a dark unknowable space filled with fog. Barring the way was a high chain-link fence with a padlocked gate, and he left the engine idling while he searched in his holdall for a keyring. A sign on the fence read STRICTLY NO ADMITTANCE: MINISTRY OF DEFENCE —

CONTAMINATED SITE. It was true that chemical weapons had once been stored here; lethal deposits still leached up through the stony soil in wet weather, of which there was plenty hereabouts. But he knew there were residues more toxic, and of newer vintage, locked away behind the fence.

Outside the car the night air smelled rusty, tainted. The man selected a key that sprung open the padlock, and leaned on the gate till it shuddered open. Back in the Saab, he disengaged the handbrake and let the car roll forwards into the forbidden space.

Parking up by a portacabin, he took the schoolbook from his holdall and positioned it deliberately on the dashboard, where it would be seen. He fetched an emergency fuel can from the back compartment of the car, glancing above him at the ramparts of notched rock, bitten out of the mountains generations ago by mechanical digger and explosive charge. At the side of the portacabin was a generator: he fed it a gallon of petrol and yanked the ripcord until it chugged into life. Flat white security floods lit up the freezing mist. In the wall of fractured slate ahead stood a double metal doorway. Stencilled on it was the word DANGER. The warning was swallowed up in the cliff face as the man undid the padlocks and slid the door open.

Moss had grown on the glass of the caged bulbs at the tunnel mouth, giving the light a soft greenish cast. At the farthest limit of the light, before the darkness swallowed everything, stood a large grey metal container, the twin of the one in the Irish schoolhouse. The man closed the sliding doors behind him and walked over to it.

His fingers trembled a little as he searched among his keys. Once he'd opened the lock on the door, he took from the holdall an inspection lamp. It didn't work at first, then as he shook the loose contact to life, shadows leaped and lunged around the tunnel walls. After a moment's hesitation, he stepped into the container.

Inside there were two chairs, one bolted to the floor, one free-standing. In the corners of the ceilings there were a couple of small cast-metal tannoy speakers. Nothing else; no independent source of light. Only white-painted walls, discoloured here and there with old stains. The man surveyed the scene, then closed the door behind him. He placed the lamp on the floor behind the bolted chair before seating himself, holdall across his knees.

The weak lamplight cast a grotesquely large shadow of the chair and its occupant on the farther wall. It was as if some great shapeshifting figure sat across from him, too massive for the claustrophobic space inside the container. What face might this shadow figure have, thought the man; what lies behind the shadow? Is there only one face behind all the shadows in the world?

The sound of his breath seemed very prominent in the enclosed space: white noise in a white room. He strove to breathe more shallowly, to disengage himself from events inside the container, to vanish, as far as was possible, from the process underway. With infinite care, he reached into the holdall and brought out the snub-nose Smith & Wesson .38 he'd toyed with on the deck of the ferry. He broke the revolver, removed the three expended casings, closed it again and spun the cylinder. With a hand that no longer shook he cocked the hammer.

Staring at the shadow, he tried to call to mind the face of the man in the schoolhouse, to separate it from all the other faces. When he pushed the revolver hard under his chin his head tilted back, and the head of the shadow that confronted him seemed to swell, to grow monstrously large and misshapen, to swallow all the light in the container. He closed his eyes so that he might not see it, but the shape was still there behind his lids. In the darkness, he thought he saw its features clearly at last.

FICTION

THE DEVIL AND THE DIVINE

Inna Effress

How will you rip away the veil of the eye, the veil
That you are, you who want to grasp the heart
Of things, hungry to know where meaning
Lies.

— Suji Kwock Kim

ON THE HEELS of a cello's moan, the aging tenor closed his eyes. His opening note rang out from the portico and across a torch-lit lawn, and silenced the patrons. Heat gnawed through their breezy silks. They'd been squirming in their white chairs arrayed in half-moons on the grass, when the singer's command stilled their beating fans. The night sky flared with shards of the past. It was August on the Island.

Clava sat with the others, entranced. There was no turning back now. It was her first chance to consider the consequences of her deed. Her face was soft and dreamy. Her eyes, cold reflective spoons. A violet petunia behind her ear did little to restrain her hair, which lashed out in all directions. If the music were to stop mid-bar, the others would take notice of her. How those blue-black kinks quivered — no, writhed! — to the tune of her agitation. The rest of her was coiled with want.

"Not just any love," the retired Doctor had warned as he slipped the oddity from its dusty box and into her restless palm. *"It's a token of forbidden love. You have to want it with a carnal desire."*

And she did.

How long before the Doctor's guarantee took effect? At any moment, her life would transform. Become unrecognizable. She fixated on the spectacle at the center of the arcade. Sure, even now, there were others remaining, a few island performers still in circulation. Sometimes, it was true, she'd confuse one for another. But none of *them* had this singer's level of *control*. There he was, his ecstatic mouth parted, a juicy black plum, facing not the quartet, not the onlookers, but at the open space in between. The singer leaned against a faded column. He was like weather, unpredictable. She could not be certain whether he avoided her gaze out of fear, or whether he was oblivious to her presence.

It was on a boat packed with strangers, without her husband, that she'd first arrived at these sultry shores. The scenery was nothing like the metropolis where she'd lived with him. Foliage mimicked extravagant plumes of mating birds. Flowers had the chitinous sheen of exoskeleton. In a hot blaze of sea, this tusk of land breached the blue waters like an ancient beast emerging from their loneliest depths. An army of giant Banyans garrisoned its shores. Now a refuge for the exiled and displaced, the Island had once been a small but thriving kingdom of tree people who had, centuries before, perished in a raging storm. All of this had been conveyed by the oarsman to Clava and the other passengers as the war-torn continent they were fleeing grew smaller behind them and they entered the warm, interlacing currents that swirled around the Island, the fabled home of the spirits of the strangler fig.

Around the concert lawn, foxfire glowed brilliant blues and greens on wild mushrooms and dead tree limbs scattered everywhere like spilled matches. The singer's final vocal chimed. It was undeniable. He had to be the one for her. She just knew. She'd been so patient. It seemed like years. Or was it only weeks? Sometimes it all struck her as unbearably strange, and she couldn't keep from erupting into her own, broken sound. He was bound to her through an unknown sense, which seized her from a distance, followed her, bled from her, and twisted her in its power from waking until sleeping.

Clava let the heaviness slip in. The woman seated next to her oozed nostalgia, though Clava didn't understand that sentiment, because this song was new. She didn't know whether to be angry or excited about the unexpected change in the program. Usually, Clava avoided staring at her neighbors, or at any of the audience; there was something unnerving about the concerts. It was never clear who, if anyone, would show up. Most kept to themselves, no interest in conversation. As if on cue, the singer's face glistened. Were these his tears, a secret summons? A sly nod to the irrevocable course she'd set in motion?

Clava tapped an excited finger against the metal of her chair and snuck a closer look at her hand. The ring was painted in miniature with a gentleman's brown eye. How lifelike it was! One shrewd eye on ivory in rose-gold, encrusted with seed pearls. The ring's weight bore into her palm. The eye's stare admired her. From every angle, the eye watched her, and only her. For the eye, only she existed. It had been so long. Clava sat taller.

DESPERATION warps judgment. Early that morning, she'd been to the Saturday antiquities market. Her outings to the Island's center had become more and more rare, but on this day, she was determined to take matters into her own hands. Who did she have to answer to? No one. She'd walked the two kilometers inland, to the old Plaza, all on her own, through crushes of flowers and ripening fruits that littered and stained the road. She'd bought the ring from the morose stall-keeper.

Specializing in Obscurities, read the sign hanging on the lintel of his kiosk, and underneath, a disclosure: *Mainland oculist, discharged.*

A bright harlequin pattern had graced his awning.

"The trick," the Doctor had said, "to ensnaring the object of your passion lies in the undying gaze of another." He'd coughed, and his sharp Adam's apple quivered too long. "Once you become the one beheld, once you are no longer the anguished beholder..." he'd stretched his slow, bony legs up onto the table with a crack, and continued, "... at that moment the transformation will take effect. It all starts with illusion."

If there was a price to pay beyond her money she didn't know it. Not yet.

AFTER the night's performance, she pulled her neckline even lower and waited out of sight, in the shadows of the bougainvillea garden. This fertile land spit flora like tumors from its soil. *A tragedy*, thought Clava, as she ripped a surprised bloom from its stalk, *for so vivid a flower to bear no scent.*

Still, paradise was approaching. It was just steps away, in the new form of her beloved. Soon, he'd be incapable of tearing his gaze from her. In the darkness, she listened to her own breathing. There were two sharp cracks as a mangrove limb snapped. Barely attached now, the limb swayed there, thick, the height of a man. The leaves at the end of the lowest branch pointed at the ground like two bound feet. Clava squinted. She gasped, then turned away, defiant. Nothing was going to spoil her chance at happiness. The ocean rumbled in the distance.

"Here I am!" She pushed through the bushes and yelped when she landed awkwardly on her weak ankle. The singer didn't seem to notice. He'd never acknowledged her in any way. She could watch him for hours. Sometimes, she did just that, lurking by the black-rock jetty at the end of her street, where he spent his time, alone. At least, she was pretty sure it was him, and not one of the others. Their forms, as of late, had seemed to shift, always shaping and re-shaping in front of her eyes. Yes, it had to be him. There was something special, something resounding, about his speech, his music. Usually he'd walk right by, singing to himself or reciting something that sounded like a poem, though she couldn't understand him, exactly, couldn't quite make out the words. She wasn't going to let him ignore her tonight.

"Over here!" She threw down the flower, whose petals she'd been shredding, and flashed the antique jewelry on her hand.

Silently, she willed him. *Look at me.* She sucked strength from the ring.

Instead of passing, he stopped. Stretched sensuously, like a snake.

"Have I got something for you," Clava waved her hand proudly. "How do you like this?"

Not quite gazing directly at her, he lifted his nose in the air and inhaled deeply. He seemed to be indulging in her newly ionized air.

"Here," she said again, and held the back of her hand out so he could get a closer look. He lifted his left arm, actually reached out! Was he going to take the ring off her finger? Her head lightened. She barely felt her mouth open and freeze that way. But he didn't touch her. Instead, he turned his closed hand over and opened it. There, on his palm, was a fig. It was the size of a heron egg, red as a shout, and prickled with hairs. She strained to see his face, his eyes. He kept his head angled down, though she thought that she saw a glimmer of something there. He seemed pleased with himself, the way his mouth turned up slightly, on just one side. Clava admitted that it could have been simply the play of shadows. If he *was* smiling, though, it was *because* of her, no matter how indirectly. That had to count for something.

He lifted the red orb to his chin, as if he was going to sniff it. Then he spit. He spit right onto the fruit. It glistened and bubbled. Under his lip, a thread of saliva gleamed. Of course, she was put off, but how could she interrupt him now? The last thing she wanted was to be untoward, to spoil the whole thing before it even started. The froth on the fuzzy surface began to thin away, the beads winking out, one by one, until a tiny pore in the fig appeared, the diameter of a thorn, and from the hole, slowly and weakly, a pale sickly yellow creature began to worm out. Before her eyes, the thing metamorphosed into a black insect with nervous wings like bridal veils. The singer pressed her quaking fingers around the fruit and the creature. Her mind a blank, she cupped her other hand reflexively over the first, like a child who has unearthed a treasure.

"For you," he said.

She opened her hand and stared at the insect, at the milky sap now seeping from the fig's opening.

Above, a bat flapped blackly to the crown of a tree. Clava squinted. Long ago, a banyan forest had emerged here, made of a single plant that spread in every direction into a latticework of connected trunks. Its flowers hid, blooming inward, sealed off inside the vast crops of figs that imprinted the landscape. These blooms waited for a wasp partner to lay her eggs inside. Then, still inside, she'd die. What began as a bat's defecated bat seed had become a sprawl of aerial root vines that snaked down and multiplied and strangled their hosts. The strangler fig. Clava felt out of breath, as if she were being strangled. An intimate symbiosis, ending and beginning in entombment. The complex circle of a fruiting life. The fig, the wasp, the bat — fulfilling their end of the barter. As Clava would.

The dwarfed wasp on her palm hummed a high pitch. Clava dropped it, along with the fruit, and took two steps back. Then, as her amazed smile turned first confused, then sour, he simply walked away, hands in pockets, reciting verses to himself, and after a while, her beloved disappeared to where the field was swallowed by a cathedral of trees.

THE following day, Clava returned to the market. She couldn't believe she'd paid so much for the worthless eye ring. Shame taunted her. She had to fight the defeat that it brought. She was going to have a word with the Doctor, demand her money back. He'd all but sworn she'd win her heart's desire. What she got was an unsatisfying exchange that left her baffled. For all she knew, her singer would never acknowledge her again.

There stood the old Doctor, stooped over his wares, hound eyes drooping. Bundles of newspaper yellowed behind him, frozen in time. This time, other patients were waiting. Some clutched rosaries to chests, or other, more exotic charms. Hope danced along their stupid faces. Inside the dim stall, she imagined she could detect their blind optimism from a distance, though they sat cloaked in shadow. The Doctor drove the others away. He quieted Clava. Then he scraped a chair from the table and offered her a plate of something that resembled dried cod, topped with strange, pungent seeds. A convocation of flies gathered the minute he set down the food.

"No, thank you," she said, lifting a ring-less hand against temptation. "I'm not hungry."

Instead, she showed him the box with her ring inside it. She thrust it across the table. Its cracked leather glinted; a gilded address embossed on its lid.

As if in response to this offering, he unlocked a small floor safe obscured by old-world globes. "A piece of history," the Doctor said.

He pressed two additional eyes into her sweating hands: one a pendant, and the other, a brooch. The first was dominating, unnerving, and just a fraction more than two centimeters. Its sclera was spongy, cork-like. The brooch's eye was pink and reptilian, a prehistoric remnant. She let him slip the third, the original, back on her finger. He started to cough again. His throat rattled oddly.

"The eye is the organ of the devil and the divine." He coaxed her back into his mystical drift. "But sometimes one is not enough."

He promised that she simply needed more. More vigor. More hunger. More eyes rooted on her. "If this is your soul's true wish, you must go home and accept what's coming. All of it." He cleared his throat. "It's only a matter of time."

His confidence had a soothing effect, and Clava became more certain than ever these relics were a bridge to another world. To a lost past. To a short-lived fashion of aristocracy, a suggestion of conquest, a hint at a lover's identity so clandestine, that only a mistress would know.

Finally, she said, "It's as if these were made just for me. Yes, I'll take them. All three."

The Doctor wrapped them with the faded newspaper.

THAT same night, Clava dabbed perfume on her neck and chest. Draped in her robe, she drew the flower from behind her ear. Black curls sprang onto her sharp cheeks. She sat on the floor, its tiles as intricate as Persian rugs. The twin arches of window yawned blackly. Under the floor lamp, she studied the pendant. She traced the mark of a crown. There was a faded inscription she couldn't divine. The Doctor had claimed a royal, an army general, had commissioned it for a mistress.

At arm's length, Clava studied it. Porous, this eye seemed stung, clouded by an onion's fumes. It was a brown receptor, impressionable as hot breath on cold glass. The pink inner corner stretched. The skin, painted to look slick, shifted so convincingly, it wasn't possible to think she was imagining things. Then, through the pinprick of a hole in the caruncle, a wet, black head squeezed out, followed by a whirring, buzzing body. Dazed, it stumbled out onto the eye's surface, dancing drunkenly on its still-unformed legs. A ferocious trembling rose in Clava's arm. She sprinkled flower-water on her neck.

She picked up the brooch and rolled it over. Under the yellow light, the eye appeared larval. It quivered and burrowed behind the soil-black pupil, which floated, unmoored, against the blue of a naked and unblinking sky. It was the mutating eye of a young god or demon. Clava turned onto her back.

Together, each vexing eye bore into her with the force of its hunger. The truth was, there was something so warm, so nice about being seen, as if they were watching her, feeding on the sight of her. It was a validation of her existence: the eager beating of her heart.

An image of her husband crept in.

"Just for a while," her husband had whispered harshly as he detached her fingers from his colonel's uniform. That was the last time she'd seen him alive, the deep lines of his face, radiating, even in repose, like the spreading crack of a mirror that returns one's reflection with fragments.

Who can say what the line is between loneliness and solitude? Once, after days on end of lonely silence, she'd lured a neighbor's son into the house, just to watch him eat cake.

Tired and disoriented, she arrayed all three eyes on her nightstand. No matter. It was useless to dwell on her marriage now. *There is love,* Clava thought as she let her head sink back, *and then, there's mortal love.*

It was early still. The splinter of moon hung low.

As usual, she waited in the dark, wondering if she'd be lucky enough to hear the singing. And there it was, she'd known it would happen. Even so, she found herself exhaling gleefully. The song from the program crept in through the windows. Usually, if she let it, the song would get louder and louder, though never so loud that she could quite decipher the words or their meanings. She sat up, and the thin sheet slipped off. She craned toward the windows in spite of herself. Two glassy cavities, thick with possibility. There was a tapping on the panes from the other side. Branches, heckled by wind. The tapping reminded her of something lost. She wasn't alarmed.

She went out to the lawn to take her seat, though not to see her love, because she listened hard, and there was another voice doing the singing tonight. Too high for a tenor. Still, she went because she wanted to see if he'd left her with another token, like that strange fruit, or something more. The scarred door slammed behind her as she ran outside. Shadows from the torches spread like thirsty roots across the unkempt grounds. In the murmuring light, the tarantula arms of trees twisted and reached. What she mistook to be a man swinging was just an animal. It had to be! She never did discover what became of her husband. Had she?

On the grass, she expected the same setup as always, chairs arranged like an amphitheater.

When she saw what was there, she slowed.

Because here was something new: a lone, white chair, dwarfed by the empty field of tall grass around it. It had been perfectly centered, and she had a clear view of the arcade. The performance was already underway. The performer's thin, piping vocals halted, then started again as soon as Clava sat. This singer was a woman. Clava had watched her on stage before, along with a handful of others, but this one was ancient as stardust while her voice was that of a little girl's. She had a round, coarse face. As she sang, she fluttered a fan against her withered chest. Even though Clava had prepared herself, disappointment won.

It was hard to keep still. "Do you know where the singer is tonight?" she interrupted. Somewhere, the night sea churned and hissed. "The other one, I mean. Silver hair, handsome. Deep voice?"

There was a shift in the air. The woman trained her cracked face on Clava. At least she had been acknowledged. Maybe this was the sign she'd been waiting for?

"I have more to show him, see? I think he

wouldn't want to miss it."

The familiar tune, the catchy one, became a chant. The chant became a single, breathy syllable. It wasn't unpleasant. It was better than nothing, wasn't it? There was something animal, inviting even, in the way this singer moved. The sureness and ease of her reminded Clava of *him*. How both singers wore the scabs of their faces like crossed thongs of tree bark.

The woman marched toward Clava. Her stringy chest proud, she chanted. Each note was a huff, an exertion. As she neared, her sounds became those of distress, panting, pushing. On the verge of a birth, her open mouth, a violet wound, a flower, fruiting, too bright and sweet. The fan clapped and clapped against the crone's tough flesh. The fan was more forceful with each strike. But when she was close enough, Clava saw that she wasn't

holding a fan at all. Instead, she was rattling what appeared to be a shell.

Now the woman's face was within reach. Her features were distorted by her wide-open mouth, which was unfortunate, because it would have been nice to see more of her, to study the details. Was there a pulse underneath that rind of skin? Would her face, in detail, seem elastic, virtuous, dazzling? Something other than a hag with a childlike voice, shining with all the promise of a sapling in spring? Clava could only guess, because there was just the mystical chasm of that mouth, like an underwater cave sucking her backwards, down and away from light, down and down into the deep, where the blind cavefish dwell, and hatch their eyeless young straight into the singular bliss that is permanent darkness.

Clava could smell the singer's breath, now

ripening, now ripened, now overripe. It was the acidic smell of fruit gone bad. A whiff of ammonia, not unlike urine. Then, without warning, her purple mouth started sputtering, more and more urgently. Breaths became gasps. Hot spray of spit splattered onto Clava's cheeks, nose, eyelids. This was uncalled for. Outrageous, even. But was it worth making a fuss? Clava squeezed her eyes closed. Confusion spooled her like a cocoon. The spit frothed and bubbled over her skin as *his* spit had over that red fig.

The itching wasn't too bad. Not at first.

She resisted the urge to wipe, to claw at her own face. She didn't want this to end, to be left all alone. Not again. All this progress, she'd been too patient to discard it over something out of her grasp. All this attention, this feeling. The swarm of spindly legs crawling over her skin strummed so passionately there was no way they could be phantoms. She refrained from crying out. She'd been waiting for this, just one touch. Now she had a whole chorus of touches. Showing restraint was the least she could do.

The singer was quiet at last. She leaned in. Clava held her breath and stared into that face, shocked to discover that the crone was blind. Two white scars, like stargazer lilies, glistened where eyes should have been. And Clava knew then what she had to do to finally be *seen*, to catch her lover's eye.

WHEN Clava finally woke, wind clawed at the afternoon sun. The itching was gone. Tiles stuck to the skin on her upper back. Something heavy weighed on her forehead, and she tore it off. It was a strange, serpentine rope, its leaves wilted, and her stomach and chest tightened with tiny cool bumps. The skirt of her nightgown was bunched up under her back, sloping her head back at an unnatural angle, so that her view was the underside of a mahogany table, a wooden spoon that had long disappeared under the porcelain stove, and the dulled blade of a knife, filmy with dried seeds, protruding recklessly from the sink counter. Sun flickered barbed messages through the branches outside.

Her memory of the previous night was a fog. With the back of a bent finger, she dug at her cheeks, chin, brows. She closed her eyes. She touched the smooth lids. What she'd witnessed was just the beginning. It was time for Clava to truly *see*.

BEHIND the beaded curtain, the Doctor was attending to another patient. Clava had grown tired of waiting. She was forced to sit with the others along the cluttered floor. Pathetic figures, mired in prayer, held their fetishes: a necklace of yellowed leopard's teeth, the jawbone of some smaller creature, a clay doll with a twisted neck, a tiny foot with a cleft hoof. She took her place among a stack of grainy photographs of national heroes, their proud chests wrapped in sashes. Her husband had torn those same heroes down from their front room wall just before his disappearance.

Beside the Doctor stood the blind, singing woman. She was smaller now, shrunken, a dwarfish familiar of her former self. She was holding a flask. Slowly at first, the beads began to clack, then crashed, accelerating until there was nothing.

Clava held out the fig left to her by the singer, "What am I to do with this?" She already knew the answer to her question. It was her destiny.

"It's just like I told you." The majestically tall oculist turned his slab of face to Clava. "You'll have your wish soon enough." A muddy paste masked his eyes.

"Once we enucleate," his deep voice soothed her, "there is no turning back. Nothing to be concerned about, perhaps only some postoperative hemorrhaging, though that is rare."

A strong odor of alcohol and sulfur seeped through every crevice. The woman, little creature, drew back the curtain to let in the light. The curtain's slanting edge held her as the light fell and fell, like violence plunging to the deepest wounds in her body.

Together, the doctor and the old woman tipped the flask of banana wine to help Clava drink. Next they bathed their hands with the wine, then rubbed the area around the Clava's eyes with leaves, which caused such a violent itching that she found herself almost longing for the cutting that was to come. Yes, it would be a relief, she thought, as they squeezed the juice from passionflower leaves directly into her eye. The Doctor, emotionless, proceeded to make the first incision.

For a moment they paused as the Doctor and the singer checked the bindings on her arms. But that was a waste. There wasn't going to be any struggle, no struggle at all.

STRANGE
TALES
Michael Eisele
THE CHILD
CEPHALINA
Rebecca Lloyd
HEAD
Carly
Holmes
The Way
Things End
Charles David
HOUSE
THE
HELPERS
Philomena van Rijswijk
DONIA
Hardy
PETALS AND
VIOLINS
TALES
D.P. Watt
tartaruspress.com

FICTION

CHILDREN OF THE ROTTING STRAW

Steve Toase

THE SKY WAS made of sticks, narrow woven and distant. Vast hurdles that covered the world. When the rains came they scented the ground with bark rot and leaf mould. I crouched to the soil catching droplets in buckets and watched the water seep out faster than the containers filled. There was not much time. The scarecrows would be coming soon.

The creaking was the first sign, a slow scraping of timber against timber as they dragged themselves through the mud. A noise that drowned out even the sound of rain. Sarah was playing across the other side of the yard.

"Time to go in now," I said, picking up the buckets. Above us sunlight slanted through the deluge and wicker clouds.

"I like it out in the rain," she said, not looking up. Around her fingers she wove daisies and meadowsweet, fingers stained with pressed petals

There were no trees to shelter under anymore. Not now the sky was sticks. The scarecrows were getting closer. Down the lane, their single feet ground and splintered along the cobbles.

"No time for that now. Come quick but steady. Bring your flowers with you, pretty things that they are. We can weave them around your mirror."

"Then when I get ready I will wear my summer garland?"

"Then you'll wear your summer garland."

Her hand was heart-sized in mine. I walked as fast as I dare. Too quick and the scarecrows would think I was running. I risked a glance to the sky. The storms always washed new ones from between the branches. There were two behind me, gazing over the garden wall, their mouths filled with rainwater, but we were soon in, the bolts across. I watched them through the window until they lost interest and moved on down the lane.

THE NEXT DAY the yarn fell. Vast strands of sheep's wool, feathered as it draped to the fields through the sky of sticks. The scarecrows stayed away. They always did when the air filled with colours. Maybe it was the sensation of the fibres upon their ragged skin, maybe the scent of lanolin on the breeze. I stood at Sarah's bedroom door.

"Get dressed. We have to harvest the sky today."

We wore thick suits stitched from shed scarecrow husks found on the lanes, stained inside with our sweat from the weight of their discarded skin. Cracked with use. Gloves to protect our hands.

Sarah followed me down the lane. I listened to her breath against the inside of her mask, and could not help checking the seams of her harvesting suit once more.

The fall was thick that day, the dense corrosive strands of wool curled upon the meadow flowers. I parked up the cart and ran my glove along the edges of Sarah's clothes.

"I made sure I sealed it properly," she said. "Just like you showed me."

I knew she was telling the truth, but I'd seen what untreated wool did to skin. How it blistered and peeled flesh. Scars that never healed.

"I like to check," I said. "You know that."

She nodded and clasped my fingers, reassuring me.

We started in the top corner, where the drystone walls met each other. I hauled the wool into the cart while Sarah wound it onto the bobbins. The yarn-fall continued throughout the day, and we continued to harvest under the slatted sun.

The message was hidden under a knot of fine madder dyed wool. A tiny thing made of paper and written in charcoal. There were only two words. 'Help Me'. I had never seen anything else arrive with the yarn, beyond scorching and scars.

Pulling the message free I folded the edges like butterfly wings and pressed it inside my glove. The dye pressed onto the paper seared my palm and I gasped. Sarah looked over, but could not see my expression behind the mask, as I could not see hers.

SHE SLEPT WELL that night. The day's harvest was more tiring than usual with several trips back and forth to the house, each time the cart loaded to the top with yarn. The colours were more varied than usual too. Madder red, onion yellow, and dogwood blue. No greens. No nettles or larkspur, but it had been a long time since either had torrented between the sticks that arced the sky.

Sat by the window, I flattened the piece of paper in one of Sarah's old books, opened it and spread the note out on the sill.

It would be a few days before the wool was dry enough to weave. For now there was nothing else to do but wait. I stared at the two words, blurred by the heat of my hand, but still legible. *Help Me*. I looked

out into the night. The scarecrows were there again, leaning against the garden wall, their arms loose by their side, showing they were awake. Watching. If they were asleep their arms would raise, waypoint stiff, showing routes no-one wanted to walk. If they saw me looking they did not react. I stared at the tear of words once more.

SARAH WOULD SLEEP through and if she woke before I returned, there was enough work to be getting on with. I watched her in her bed for a few moments, curled up under abandoned tapestries we had not finished. Half formed unicorns and knights in loose weave. Edges frayed from the lack of finishing. The absence of one or another colour needed to complete a design.

I glanced out the window. The scarecrows had left. Now there was time to wait. I sat in the dark, the stench of wool drifting in from the weaving shed. She would be fine if I left for a couple of days. She would be fine.

The scarecrows were easy to track, twinned ruts from their single feet as they dragged themselves in parallel to their nest.

They leaned against each other while they slept, shoulder against shoulder, their bulbous faces turned outward and toward the sky, arms outward pointing to places that did not exist.

No-one ever saw them return to the place beyond the sky of sticks, but everyone saw the beds left empty of children.

I walked light, circling the meadow grass where they stood. Their expressions did not change between rest and wake. They did not scent me. Did not react to my presence at all. I moved in closer, but kept at arm's reach. I'd not seen scarecrows attack, but I'd seen the results. Circular splintered wounds piercing rotting corpses. The struggling bodies, still alive, hoisted on loops of yarn, their skin scorched and scraped.

I moved quick. I could when I needed to. Slid

the flensing knife into the back of the first scarecrow and stood back as mould-spotted straw spilt out. The second scarecrow woke, trying to turn to where I crouched. I ducked under the arms, escaping the grip that would not open once closed. My knife flicked up, slicing away button thread, then the stained shirt underneath. All the time its stuffing continued to empty it continued to reach for me, until there was so little left it crumpled to the ground.

I'd never gutted a fresh one, normally harvesting the skins from roadkill or husks found out beyond the fields. Reaching into the wounds I dragged out vast handfuls of straw, trying to ignore the urge to vomit as it crawled across my skin. Pushing my hands into the head I carved out the inside and tipped the seeds into the soil, crushing them below my heel.

Once empty both skins fitted in a rucksack, compressed as I tightened the straps. For a moment I thought about torching the insides left scattered around the clearing. Burning the straw and the seeds and the flesh, but I did not want to remain there anymore. Above me the sky of sticks sliced the moon into razors of light.

IT WAS NORMAL for a yarn fall at night to follow one during the day. I did not return to the house to check on Sarah. If she woke then my words of explanation would not be effective.

Instead I sheltered in the weaving shed and slid myself into the scarecrow skin. The inside was still damp, reeking of winter haystacks, dying rats and putrid fruit spoiling in the fields. A smear of flesh stuck to my lips and pushed against my tongue. I hooked it out and watched the beetles crawl away over the stone floor.

THE YARN DRAPING from the sky was thigh thick. Wide enough to bear my weight.

I knew the husks could keep the corrosive dyes at bay while we harvested and lowered the fibres into the fixing pits, but to protect me as I climbed? There was no certainty, and for my hands to start burning halfway up? Either the fall or the scalds would do for me.

I chose the thickest strand I could find. Even in the dark the vivid purple of hibiscus glowed. I reached up and wrenched the yarn. It held. I wrapped my legs around, and dragged myself up.

There had been something in the curl of the letters that looked familiar, a recognition that intensified when I placed the note beside Sarah's schoolbooks.

My daughter was up above the sky of sticks. Not my Sarah as she was now, asleep and unaware, but my Sarah in the future. Maybe the scarecrows would take her from my care in two hours, or two weeks or two years. I did not know for certain. The only thing I knew at that moment was I had to rescue this Sarah. I held the note tight, even as I clung to the yarn.

Though the fresh scarecrow skin kept the dyes away from mine, the fumes still seeped in through the mouth, stinging my nose and eyes. I tried to hold my breath. The hand over hand climb needed more air than I cared for and so I had to hope that the steam rising from under my hands was less corrosive in the air than to touch.

The climb was long and didn't get any easier. Above me the sky got closer. So near they were no longer sticks, or branches, but vast trunks, woven together. Each new growth wrapped around the last. The yarn draped down through the gaps. Hundreds of them like vines of colour, burning away the bark to the heartwood below. The blood of the trees stuck to the second skin I wore and seared scars into the hands and arms. I ignored the scent of cooking meat and continued to pull myself up, dragging myself around the rough branches.

GLANCED DOWN through the sky of sticks to the ground below. I could just make out the fields. A patchwork of land that smeared at the edges.

I rolled onto my back then sat. Every metre of the sky of sticks was covered in bark huts, silver birch and oak plated together into walls and roofs. Some were barely big enough to fit a single person, others so vast they obscured the second sky above. From the larger huts cables of yarn evacuated through open doors, finding the spaces between to drape to the ground below. The smaller ones were quieter, doors bolted from the outside, most attached to the larger houses like tumours. Between everything moved the scarecrows, their single legs uneven and unbalanced on the rough trunks underfoot.

I waited, letting my breath still as much as I dare while I recovered. While I decided where to start looking. The air itself stung my eyes. Everything floated through tears and sweat.

The scarecrows ignored me as they walked their rounds, fixed expressions unchanging, mouths always open. Even if they saw they seemed not to care that my legs did not narrow to a single point or that my chest moved.

I leant forward to stare back to where my home should be. I watched the nearest hall opened, thousands of strands of yarn pushing across the wooden floor. Moving slowly I walked up to the door and leant around the corner. Wherever Sarah was it was not in there.

Scarecrows stood around roof high wheels twisting wool, bringing fibres together into vast strands before it fed out of the door to fall like solid rain. There were no people, no-one taking breath, just the children of the rotting straw.

If Sarah was not in the spinning hall, she must be nearby. Near enough to slide the note between the fibres that passed under the scarecrows' fixed stares.

I took the first hut, opening the door with care.

The room was tiny and reeked of rotten meat. The figure inside was not a scarecrow, not anything at all anymore but food for the thousands of insects that swarmed over mould-covered bones. I moved closer, trying to ignore the stench. At least these scents didn't scorch my mouth.

The girl slumped forward over a pile of wool, the fleece itself sodden and growing its own forest, the line between person and product of no consequence to the creatures that feasted there.

Sliding my skin-covered fingers through the hair, I turned the strands over, searching for something familiar. A perfume or knot to tell me this was my daughter. There was nothing.

I heard scarecrows passing the door and waited until they had gone. They did not speak to each other, so I did not worry about them asking me questions. Maybe they scented the rain-ruined straw. I hoped enough was smeared within my disguise to distract them from my blood and bone.

Once they passed I moved onto the next, empty of everything except a single pitcher of water, and the third, crammed so high with the dead that the flies blacked out any light.

The fourth hut was larger, stood on its own a slight distance from the spinning room. From inside I heard a scraping noise, the sound of fine combs meeting each other and pulling away. Standing outside I listened until I heard breath and opened the door.

She was older than the Sarah in the world below, and the look of fear she wore upon seeing me aged her more. I reached behind my head and unstitched the scarecrow's face.

"You got the note," she said. There was exhaustion in her voice, her fingers bleeding. In her hands she held dried teasels, the spikes thick with off-white fibres.

"We need to get out of here before the scarecrows notice," I said, unpacking my bag and holding out the second skin. "Put this on."

I looked at the tiny amounts of wool in the room, small bins full of carded fibres ready to be spun. I tried to imagine the amount needed for a single length. I pictured all the huts I would not find with stolen children. I pictured how big the sky was, and despite the need to rescue my daughter I wept for all those who would not be saved.

"I can't wear that, Mum," she said, shrinking back against the far wall.

"Then I cannot save you," I said. "I cannot get you away from this place and back to the land below."

She was at least ten years older than the Sarah I'd left sleeping below, and I had to bite my tongue to stop myself asking about what filled in time between the two daughters I now had.

She turned to face the wall and I fastened up the back, watching the skin knit itself together. Though she stared out of the face, the eyes were not hers, but those of the scarecrow I'd ambushed.

"We have to leave soon," she said, her voice sounding fearful even when muffled. "They will come soon for the wool. They're always coming for the wool."

I nodded, tying my own disguise back in place, hiding any fear I might hold myself. I reached out a hand and she took it with a fist far bigger than a heart. I opened the door and waited.

THE YARNS WERE still falling to the ground below. Finding the vivid purple strands was not hard, and I went first, wrapping myself around, clasping it as I would clasp Sarah when we were safe.

She followed and we slid back down to the ground, away from the sky of sticks. The scarecrows paid us no attention.

Returning was faster than the climb, the friction of the fibres burning against our covered limbs. I kept glancing up to check Sarah was still above me, and tried not to flinch every time I saw a raggedy man following, reminding myself it was my offspring, my flesh, no matter what disguise she wore.

Reaching the ground, we both tumbled away, toppling in the meadow grass until we came to rest, vertical and upright.

THIS WAS THE time for reassuring words, the time to embrace her and tell her everything would be ok. That no-one would take her again. That not a single fibre of wool needed to pass through her hands. I spoke the words but none came. There was no sound. Not a single syllable no matter how loudly I tried to shout. Reaching around the back of my head I searched for the stitched seam to free myself from this dead skin.

I looked over at Sarah. She was pointing at my legs. I did not look down, but pressed my fattened fingers into my mouth. Felt the rotten straw within. Now, when there was nothing else to do, I lowered my gaze and stared. Sarah's legs were gone, replaced with a single wooden pole, stained and splintered.

I DID NOT know where else to go. Sarah followed, as trapped as I was. She had no other destination, and kept pace as I dragged myself through the lanes, and over the cobbles.

The younger Sarah was playing across the other side of the yard.

"Time to go in now," my earlier self said, picking up the buckets. Above us the sunlight slanted through the rain and the wicker clouds.

"I like it out in the rain," the younger Sarah said, not looking up. Around her fingers she wove daisies and meadowsweet, her fingers stained with pressed petals.

FICTION

HER VOICE, UNMASKED

Suzan Palumbo

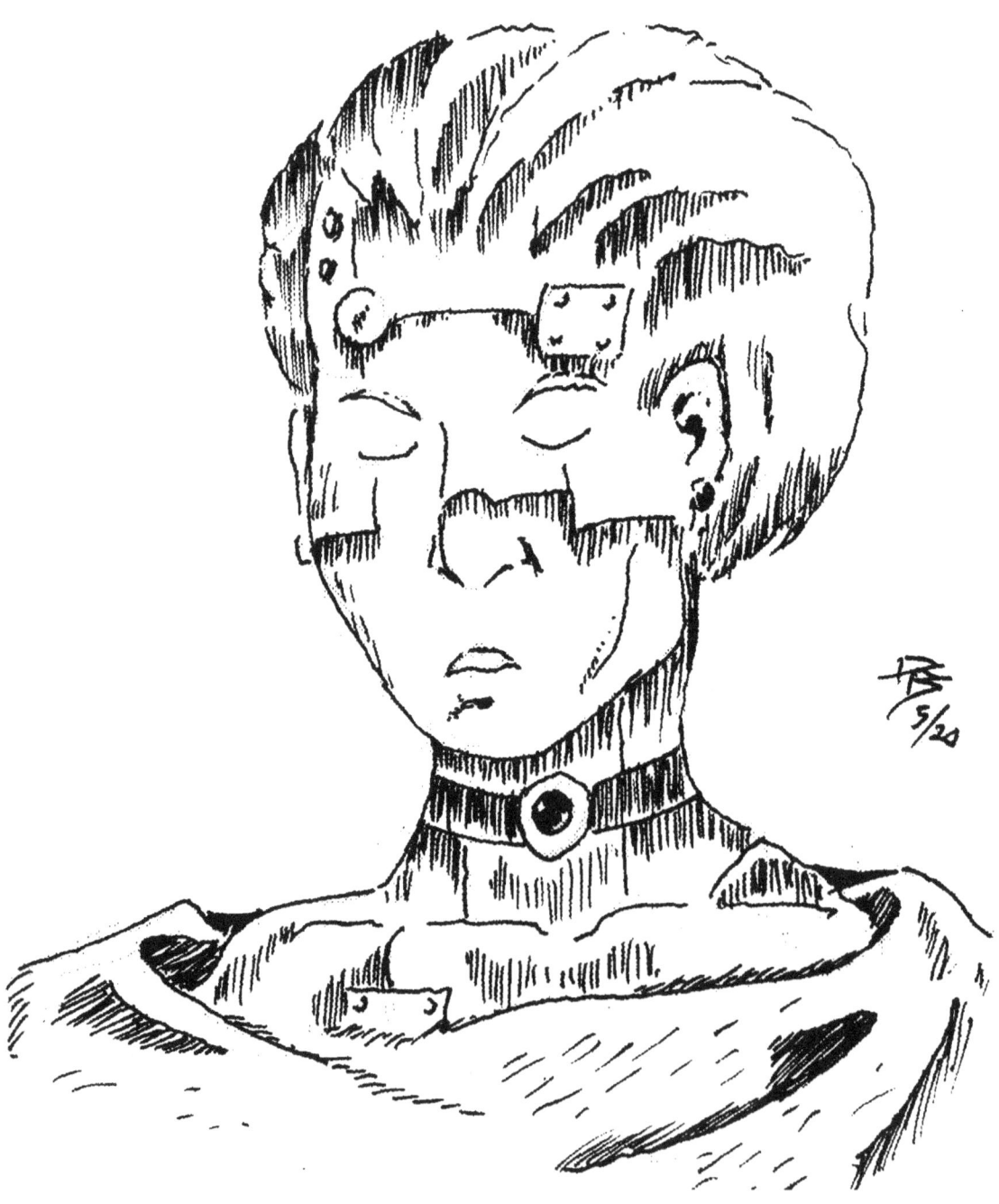

JUSTINE'S VOICE *breaks against the vaulted ceiling of the Opera House. The gas lamps ringing the stage reflect light off her faceplates each time her mouth opens and closes around the notes. Her only accompaniment is the whip crack of the Maestro's demands: "Again! Again!"*

The Maestro has winched her vocal chords taut with an awl as she's gained proficiency over the past two years: Contralto, Mezzo-Soprano, Soprano. He's tuned her up, though she isn't an instrument fashioned out of glue and twisted sheep's gut by an Italian great. He's created her himself using boards and gears in his subterranean workshop tucked into the bowels of the theatre.

"Higher, longer, clearer. Sing!" His hands chop and slice the air. Dark locks tossed over his severe brow, he is frenetic. Obsessive. And, at her debut tomorrow night, Justine will be the conduit of his genius.

She inhales, rubber diaphragm flexing, internal bellows filling to the edge of bursting. Air rushes in. She must imbue it with light and rapture before it spools from her artificial lips into the empty auditorium.

She repeats his instructions internally before she begins: *Hold the breath for a second and then release.*

The note pours out of her. Overtones, smooth. Creamy. The metallic buzz of her articulators is barely audible after two years of relentless practice. Yet, a faint twang remains, colouring the sound resonating in the room, until her air is spent and the theatre falls silent. She glides her hinged jaw shut and looks to the Maestro.

His elegant fingers cover his ears. He is shaking his head, a red tint staining his pale face. She has learned this means he is angry with her.

"No. Justine. The audience must be moved, you

must hold them rapt." His words are staccatoed. Restrained. "They know an automaton can hit the notes. They expect nothing less." His mouth twists into a sneer. "They've come to the opera to lose themselves, to escape from their petty bourgeois lives. Can your voice thrill them, Justine? Can you break their hearts?"

Justine nods, re-imprinting her boards with subtler shades of meaning. Her purpose isn't to mimic a soloist. But how can she distill the depths of joy or despair into a simple puff of air and transfer their weight to an audience?

"Yes, Maestro," she answers.

She sees from the slackening set of his face that he is unconvinced. The tickets have been sold, the playbills displayed. She must succeed. His triumph or tragedy rests squarely on her shoulders.

"Come back tomorrow morning. We'll try one last time." He waves her away. She leaves him on the stage, his head bowed. Deflated.

JUSTINE ASSISTS AT the ballet school adjacent to the Opera in the afternoons. Automatons have no need for rest and the Maestro, at the request of the Opera's proprietors, has graciously permitted the free use of his creation for educational purposes. She is, most often, in the senior class: a group of thirteen teenaged girls, clad in soft artificial-pink tights and one-pieces. Feet gloved in canvas slippers.

Coiled energy and trigger-released grace, they titter before Madame Garnier, the ballet Mistress, enters and stand at posture perfect attention when she arrives. Once a principal dancer herself, Madame Garnier's demeanor is cool, fluid. A rope braid clamped tightly to her scalp, her pallid eyes are chisel sharp. She stands at the front of the class, still as a marble statue, appraising the dancers.

Madam Garnier uses Justine to demonstrate choreography and pinpoint the unfocused alignment of each dancer. Justine, unlike the girls, can hold each pose with aplomb eternally; her metal limbs clicking into place — immune to the organic seizing of cramps or muscle spasms as she pirouettes before the class.

No dancer studies Justine's performances with more zeal than Lise, who at seventeen, is the oldest girl in the class. Justine senses Lise's eyes shadowing her, sees the girl's lips moving soundlessly — measuring each beat, internalizing every extension of Justine's legs and arms. Justine has come to think of this as Lise's mantra; her silent prayer to the bal-

let Gods.

Today, Madame Garnier has an announcement. "Girls! The Ballet Master needs four of you for his new production of *Crepuscolo!*" Justine notices a change in Lise's face, a slight arch of her eyebrows; an almost imperceptible bounce of her knee. Madame Garnier reads the names of the chosen. The quartet beams as they collect their bags and the Mistress ushers them to the main studio. Lise's eyebrows fall, tugged by a riptide beneath her composed exterior. The significance of the shift is just beyond Justine's understanding.

Afterwards Madame Garnier returns and Justine watches Lise and the remaining girls work through the choreography for the Fall recital. She cannot sense the heartbreak that mars the twist of Lise's waist or the turn of her ankles. Lise throws her body into the routine as if the fate of the world were balanced on the precise angle of her arabesque. When class is over, Lise is left alone with Justine.

"Can I assist you with anything, Lise?" Justine asks as she tidies the studio.

"No. There isn't anything you can do, Justine." Lise averts her eyes, refusing to make contact.

"Will you be using the studio for extra practice today?

"Practice is pointless." There's a slope blunting Lise's shoulders that wasn't there before.

Justine slants her head forty-five degrees. "Practice makes perfect." Justine has had success with this line of reasoning with dancers in the primary divisions. Lise's smile in response is soft, almost blurred. It's a smile Justine's seen before, on the older women who scrub the opera. *Sorrowful? Disappointed?* She cannot distinguish between the two.

"They don't want perfect. They want *transcendent.*" Lise pulls off her slippers and unravels her hair. "But, there is something you could do for me, if you'd still like to?"

In the pause before she answers, Justine considers the artery thrumming in Lise's throat. She can hear Lise's breath hitch in her lungs as she exhales. Justine holds herself back from touching the girl — from placing her hand softly against Lise's collar bone and saying: *Help me feel the music.*

"Yes, Lise?" Justine says.

"Would you sing for me?"

"Would you like to hear the aria I am to perform tomorrow night? The Maestro wrote it especially for me."

"No." Lise shakes her head. There's a crease in her brow. "Sing me something else. Something about failure."

Lise sits on the bench along the wall and folds her hands neatly in her lap. Justine takes position at center. She shuffles through the boards of music the Maestro has provided her. The word failure doesn't factor into any of his entries. Then, she trips over a song board she's imprinted herself. A song sung by one of the cleaning women.

She begins tentatively — the lyrics lament the Queen of the dark side of the Moon; a Queen who gambles on her lover and loses everything.

Her voice finds purchase in the second stanza. It amplifies, spilling into the studio — unraveling, silvery and clear. But, she cannot capture the emotion behind the words. *Is it regret? No, something different, the heart of it is...shattered.* She visualizes the image of Lise pirouetting — transposed on the desolate lunar mare, clouds of charcoal-coloured dust scattering with each rotation. It is cold and lonely. There is nothing warm on the Moon.

When Justine is finished, Lise's eyes are redrimmed. Her cheeks damp. Justine sits next to her.

"I am sorry, Lise. I meant to assist you, not make you unhappy."

Lise throws her hands around Justine's neck and kisses her cool cheek. "That was perfect." She wipes her face and exits the studio.

Justine remains on the bench repeating the word "transcendent" before returning to the main Opera House to wind down.

THE MAESTRO IS unshaven the next morning; his back is as rigid as his baton. He is older than the Ballet Master, just over fifty and while she cannot feel attraction, the cleaning women have informed Justine that he is unconventionally handsome.

He'd seemed pleased with Justine's progress, at first. He'd laughed and took time to detail his illustrious career as a tenor; his royal audiences, his unmatched potential. "I pushed myself too hard, Justine. I damaged my voice," he'd said, a pall darkening his face. "I had to take music students at the Opera just to eat."

Justine watched the spark return to his eyes when he'd explained how he'd discovered a flute playing automaton in a travelling show one evening. "I knew how I'd triumph." He'd smiled wide when he'd told her. He procured the automaton on credit from the Opera's proprietors, promising them he'd build a soloist with a range beyond human capability. Then, he set to work deconstructing the flute player, studying it parts; creating Justine.

Pressure from the Opera's proprietors began to grow. Justine had overheard their demands: "When will the machine be ready, Maestro?" "We cannot fund your mechanical hobbies indefinitely. Where is the return on our investment?" One morning, they'd delivered an ultimatum: Justine would open the fall concert season or the Maestro would repay his debts and leave disgraced.

"I'm running out of time," he'd said to her after the proprietors left.

And as her debut has drawn closer, the Maestro's agitation has increased. Nothing she sings appeases him. She's rehearsed his aria countless times but cannot pinpoint what her performance lacks; what crucial knowledge she is missing.

The Maestro's hands are raised at his podium now, waiting for Justine to take her mark. She stands in place and they begin. Her voice soars, startling the cleaning women amid their dusting of the baroque relief-covered balconies.

"Uninspired!" His scream cuts her off. Fills the theatre. He scatters his sheet music on the floor, lunges towards her, awl in hand. "The claims I've made. They will laugh me out of the city." His voice is fractured. His jaws crunch together so tense they look as hard as metal, like hers.

"I'm sorry, Maestro."

"You don't know what sorry is. Useless bucket of pins!"

"I — "

He slams the awl's handle into Justine's face below her left eye. The dull clank of wood against metal jolts the cleaning women into a flurry of spit polish. Justine brings her hand up to her face plates. There's a shallow crater on her left cheek.

The Maestro glares at her. Dashes the awl to the floor. "See what you've made me do? Pick these papers up and fix your face." He turns, storming off the stage. "Be on time tonight. We wouldn't want to be late for my grand failure," he yells behind him.

On her hands and knees, Justine picks up the Maestro's score and reorders it before placing the sheets back on his stand. She retrieves the awl. She imagines herself as the Moon Queen, surveying her lost lunar kingdom as she stands on the stage.

The cleaning women continue their work in silence. None dare criticize the Maestro's methods.

"**W**HAT HAPPENED, Justine?" Lise asks after class. Justine considers the tone *of Lise's voice. Is it worried? No, concerned.*

"My singing was unsatisfactory. The Maestro hit me with my tuning awl."

Lise recoils at the words, pressing her hands to her own face as if the Maestro had hit her instead of Justine. "He shouldn't hit you."

"His reputation is at stake. The playbills advertise him as, 'The Maestro who made a clockwork heart tremble with a voice of flesh and blood.' If I fail, he will have failed."

Lise touches Justine's cheek. "Does it hurt?" She bites her bottom lip, almost as if to prevent herself from saying more.

"I'm incapable of pain, Lise."

Lise is quiet for a moment. She pulls her hand away. Her eyes trace the depression on Justine's face. "I'm leaving school at the end of this term," she says.

"Discontinuing ballet?" Justine asks.

"Yes."

Justine nods, uncertain of whether she should ask Lise to explain why. "Will you attend the performance tonight?"

"I wouldn't miss it, Justine."

"I am not adequate by human standards."

Lise's words are feathery, unfocused. "Do you like singing, Justine?"

Justine has never encountered this question before. Her clockwork surges trying to understand.

"Yes. I think I do like singing."

"Then sing for yourself tonight. Not for the Maestro. Just for you."

"The Maestro will not be pleased."

"It's your voice, Justine. Make the song your own."

IN THE EARLY evening, the costumers arrive to dress Justine. She's been allotted the use of a personal dressing room for this night only.

The Maestro has chosen a Grecian-style gown of black silk chiffon, a supple contrast to the hard lines of her alloy body. Once dressed, the costumers affix a Venetian colombina to her face using a black ribbon. It hides the disfigured plate she hasn't had time to repair. The gold filigree on the mask is like delicate frost. Her angular jaws have been left exposed. Naked.

The costumers survey her, nodding in agreement. The Maestro's vision is, "otherworldly," "arresting."

They leave her to collect her thoughts and warm up her voice, as is customary with soloists before a performance.

Sing for yourself.

Lise's words press on Justine's mind. *Myself.* Justine's the Maestro's creation and yet…she looks at herself in the mirror and cannot understand the reflection she sees. The mask isn't right. Something is amiss.

She takes the awl and holds it against her thigh. Someone will notice if she alters her costume now. She will wait until she is alone backstage. A few minutes later, the stagehands arrive to escort her to her mark.

They leave her on a platform beneath the main stage that will elevate her through a trap door into the theatre above. In the darkness, she undoes the knot in the ribbon of the colombina and tosses it aside. She uses the awl to pry her face plates from the metal frame of her head and tosses them alongside the mask. Unconstrained, her internal workings spring out. Clots of rubber and a mass of the Maestro's handmade gears and vacuum tubes are visible above her jaws. She inhales; her insides shift. Her vocal articulators open up, unfurling, stretching up her throat and down to her flexible diaphragm. Her inner workings settle in her chest, grounding her.

The intro music swells. The elevator ascends, carrying her upwards through the open trap door into the glowing light above. The audience gasps. *Horror? Shock?* Perhaps it is both.

The Maestro's eyes flare like the gas lamps dotting the edge of the stage. His jaw clenches, mechanical.

Justine searches the multitude of powder-caked faces for Lise high into the stadium seating. She spots her despite the blinding glare of the chandelier lighting the theatre.

Sing for yourself.

Justine inclines her head towards Lise. Tonight, she will sing for them both.

The Maestro raises his hands. The performance will go on. There is a moment of silence.

The song erupts from her, flooding the auditorium.

This isn't the Maestro's Aria. It is a fantasia; an improvisation of Justine's own creation: The Moon Queen's Triumph.

Her tone is like a warm sickle. Curve sharpened and unsheathed. She is the Moon Queen. Her treasonous lover has split her heart in twain but the Moon is hers. No one will take it from her.

The audience shudders as the melody slices into them. Smooth caesuras drag them forward to the edges of their seats. They are rapt. Justine's hooked into the gaps between their ribs and rocketed them into interstellar space. They are on the lunar plain and she has found the edge between soloist and audience that tapers to stardust and incandescence.

She crescendos. The penultimate note reverberating through the chandelier above them and resonating in their hearts as the Moon Queen banishes her treasonous paramour and reclaims her throne. Victorious.

Justine falls silent.

The theatre is breathless. The gas lamps go down.

The audience explodes into thunderous ovation. Roses and handkerchiefs sail to the stage as Justine is lowered through the trap door back into the under belly of the theatre.

The stage hands whisk her to her dressing room. Frenzy. Electricity. She is to see no one except the Maestro.

He comes to her hours later.

"Well done Justine." But the bend of his features doesn't match his words. He isn't happy like she'd thought he'd be. He hands her the colombina and dented face plates she discarded. She takes them and puts them on the dressing table.

"Thank you, Maestro. It was a song I created myself."

"It wasn't the aria I'd planned." There's an edge to his voice.

"No, Maestro." She puts her hands up in front of her in anticipation of his quick temper. "I thought that if I performed a song I could feel, I would do your training justice."

"You thought?" He's taken aback. "A song you could feel?" His voice has become scalpel sharp.

"Yes. Heartbreak, in this case. The audience appeared to like it." He stares at her, appraising, like Madame Garnier.

"They did. It was a complete success." His speech trails off, almost as if he's thinking, the gears in his head turning. For a moment it seems like his mind is somewhere far away and not in the room with her. When he refocuses there's heat in his eyes. "Come with me down to the laboratory. Bring your face plates. I will repair them."

Justine careens at his abrupt change in demeanor. She follows him, nonetheless. He is, after all, her creator. She mustn't question him.

He leads her through the corridors of the Opera House. The dim lit lower levels are ghost silent. They descend to the very foundations of the building where they arrive at a heavy wooden door encased in an ancient stone archway. The Maestro heaves the door open and a staircase fans downward into a damp cavern. He leads on into the gloom, effervescent nitre painting a ghastly glow on his profile. The air is foul, completely divorced from the perfumed opulence of the theatre above. Justine remembers this passage. She'd climbed these very steps when the Maestro brought her up to the Opera House. This is the place of her birth, where she'd first become aware.

They reach the bottom of the stairs and are confronted by another ancient wooden door. The Maestro swings it open. She follows him into his clinical laboratory.

He takes the face plates from her hands and points to the metal table in the center of the room. "Lie down," he commands.

She does as she's directed. He turns his back to her, tosses the plates onto a work table and rummages through the drawers in a heavy oak cabinet.

"You are right, Justine. Your performance was sublime. We will be embarking on a world tour."

"A tour?"

"Yes. To mark my triumph. My conquest over the human voice and the artistic spark." He turns to face her, a pair of pliers in his hands. His expression is inscrutable. He comes over to the table and stands above her, looking directly into her mechanical eyes.

"Will you use those to fix my plates?" she asks. He does not seem to hear her question.

"You are special, Justine. Not like other automatons, like that silly flute player — a lifeless recording device with a face. I knew I could make you sing. Make your voice fly." He crosses his arms, savouring his brilliance like a full-bodied port. "Of course, I had to invent all of the mechanisms, boards and clockwork by myself. No small feat. But true art is more than the sum of its parts. You needed something more. A little magic." There's an unfamiliar smile on his lips. An involuntary shudder passes through her metal frame. *A shiver?*

He leans over her, his face a few inches from her exposed tubes and rubber lips. When he speaks next, his voice is baritone. Soft. "I breathed life into

you, Justine. Before I completed the final connections and wound you up, I put my lips on yours and filled your bellows with music. In and out, we respirated together. Your first breath was mine. It's me they loved, tonight." He stands up and stares down at her, watchful of the effect his revelation has on her.

Her gears churn. *It's your voice, Justine. It's me they love, Justine.* The contradictory sets of knowledge batter against each other in her rubber connectors. One of them is invalid. *Which one is incorrect?* She discards them both and returns to the only question she's been able to answer with any certainty. *Do you like singing, Justine?* She takes a breath on the table, her chest cavity filling. When she exhales, her answer is unequivocal: *Yes.*

The Maestro's mouth is a thin, firm line. He continues, unaware of the burgeoning rebellion developing in the metal skull on the table. "And now that I know I've succeeded, I need to ensure you do as directed. No more 'songs of your own creation.' No more 'ability to choose.'"

His voice is hard again, masked. His jaw is rigid. He puts one hand on Justine's forehead, pinning her down and bends over her exposed tubing. He jabs the needle points of the pliers into the sides of a component just below her right eye socket. A board that assists with decision making, Justine intuits. He yanks upward, jerking her head off the table and banging it back down. *It's my voice. Make the song my own.*

The words fire through her as the mechanism begins to give way. She clamps her hand down on the Maestro's wrist and forces the pliers from her face, pushing him back from her and down onto the floor. Under the vice of her metal joints, the delicate bones in his wrist shift, on the threshold of braking. He drops the pliers. He is on his knees.

"Justine. Stop. Stop." *Rage.* Justine recognizes rage searing beneath the dense agony in his voice. A heavy sensation courses through her. *Pity.* She lets go. Steps back, looking down at him.

"I've hurt you, Maestro. For that, I am sorry. I do not want to go on a world tour. I'd like to remain here at the Opera House and assist with the ballet school."

"The ballet school?" He spits at her, incredulous, while massaging his wrist. "What do you think will happen when you wind down? I'll disembowel you. Scoop out the rubber from that bucket brain and remake you. You are a shell."

Justine angles her head. "That certainly is possible Maestro, though it would not be wise. Your work, supreme genius, reduced to a metal hull. I cannot perform without the ability to feel. Where will the evidence of your great triumph be?"

He scrambles towards the pliers and stands to face her. Her logic is air tight. "This is how you repay your creator?" There is an arrogant shine in his eyes, dark and malignant that shadows something pointed. Deeper. An emotion Justine never recognized before. Fear. The Maestro is terrified of losing control of her.

"Maestro. You've given me a voice, for that I am grateful. Any Opera House would gladly welcome you. But if you attempt to take away my ability to choose again, I will break both your hands." She wrenches the pliers from him.

He tries to grab her arm but she latches onto his wrists and squeezes until the bones crack beneath her metal fingers. He is on his knees again, begging. "Justine, Please. You are my life's work. There's nothing else."

She shakes her head and lets go of his hands, stepping around him to retrieve her dented face plate from his work bench. She leaves the Maestro writhing, cradling his hands. "I'm sorry," she whispers as she exits the laboratory. Hollow curses follow her as she traverses the caverns, ascending back the way she came into the light of the Opera House.

THE NEXT MORNING, there are whispers among the cleaning women. The Maestro had an accident. His beautiful hands are mangled. The Opera's proprietors recovered him from his laboratory, delirious. He'd bequeathed Justine to the Opera as repayment for his debts in a mumbled apology when they'd found him, and then begged them to let him create a more perfect soloist. He passed into unconsciousness before he'd heard their answer.

His performances have been cancelled. The playbills removed. All tickets are set to be refunded.

"I was unaware anything occurred. I had already shut down for the night," Justine answers, when she is wound up in the morning and questioned.

THE WHISPERS HAVE not died down by the time Justine makes her way to the ballet studio in the afternoon. She has reattached the damaged face plates to her head. She's decided not to repair them. She doesn't want to cover it up.

Lise is early for class.

"I saw you sing, Justine," she says. "It was beautiful."

"Thank you, Lise." Justine responds. "Did you think it was…transcendent?"

Lise's smile is brilliant and crisp. "Yes. Justine. You were transcendent. It made me think…think about staying."

"Staying on with ballet?" Justine asks.

"Yes."

"Why, Lise?"

Lise is silent a moment. "It's who I am, Justine," she says.

Justine's lips curve into a smile. "Yes, I know how you feel," she says.

FICTION

YOU CAN'T SAVE THEM ALL

Ian Rogers

SHE WAS PRETTY, all things considered.

Veronica didn't have all the details yet — the police had dropped the girl off only an hour ago — but you didn't have to be a children's aid worker to see she had been through hell.

The dark-rimmed eyes with the thousand-yard stare. The thin, malnourished cheeks. The long, greasy hair that hadn't been washed in days or weeks.

And yet there was a glow about the girl, an air of quiet defiance that suggested even though she had been abused, possibly in several different ways, she still retained a spark of innocence. A piece of herself that remained untouched, untainted.

Veronica didn't see that glow very often — perhaps one in ten of the kids she had encountered during her almost twenty years with the Brooklyn Office of Children and Family Services — but she always felt a pang of relief when she did. She knew the day she stopped seeing that glow was the day she'd have to pack it in and go find another line of work.

The girl was sitting in a plastic contour chair next to her desk. Veronica didn't have an office, but then neither did any of the other case workers here at Brooklyn OCFS. It was the same excuse: not enough space, not enough money. Veronica didn't mind. The maze of cubicles, desks, and file cabinets made it feel she was working in a police squad room or a newspaper bullpen. All the noise and activity helped to distract from the emotionally draining work that took place here every day.

"What's your name, sweetie?"

The girl didn't say anything, just continued to stare off into the distance.

"It wouldn't happen to be Honey Boo Boo, would it?"

Nothing. Not even a giggle.

"Okay," Veronica said. "That's cool. You're the strong, silent type. I can dig that."

Still nothing.

"Would you like a hot chocolate?"

The girl shrugged her bony shoulders. That was something, at least.

"Would you like a coffee?" Veronica tried.

Another shrug.

"How about getting me one?" Veronica said.

That got a reaction. The small head turned toward her and the eyes in their smudged sockets locked onto hers.

Veronica held her mug out to the girl. "Coffeemaker's right over there in the corner. One cream, three sugars. Chop, chop, kid."

The girl kept staring at her, then the corners of her mouth turned up in the smallest of smiles. "Get it yourself!" she chirped, loud enough to make a few heads pop up over the nearby cubicles. One of those heads belonged to Dee Dee Meadows, who sat in the neighbouring cube.

"Keep it down, will ya?" Dee Dee said, smiling. "Can't you see the monster's trying to sleep over here." She turned her head to the right as a plush Cookie Monster doll appeared over the top of the cubicle wall next to her. "Cookie!" Dee Dee cried in a pretty good imitation of the Cookie Monster's voice. "Want COOKIE!" Dee Dee shook her head and frowned at the girl. "See what you've done now? I can't get this monster back to sleep unless I give him a cookie."

"That's not a monster!" the girl said.

Dee Dee turned the doll so they were looking at each other. "Are you sure?" she said. "He looks like a monster to me." The doll disappeared behind the wall. "And these look like cookies." She brought up a bag of Oreos. "You want one?"

The girl nodded and Dee Dee tossed her an Oreo. She looked at Veronica. "You want one, too, or maybe something stronger?"

"Reggie's? Later?"

"Sounds good," Dee Dee said, and ducked back behind the wall.

"You've got spunk, kid," Veronica said, turning back to face the girl. "I think you're going to go far in this business."

The girl gave her a look that contained equal parts confusion and amusement. "You're different," she said.

"And you're short," Veronica shot back. "Glad we got that out in the open. Now how about we move on to something else. Like your name."

The kid lowered her head again, and Veronica thought, *Dammit, I lost her.* But then the girl muttered something, too low to be heard.

"What was that, honey?"

She muttered it again. Veronica leaned forward, straining to hear.

"Sue?"

The girl's head snapped up, the air of defiance around her blazing now. "Susan!" she shouted. "Not Sue!"

Veronica bit down on the smile that wanted to spread across her face. Instead she nodded grimly. "Susan it is. My name is Veronica."

She offered her hand. The girl started at it for a moment, then reached out timidly and shook it.

Cold, Veronica thought. *Her hand is so cold. How long was she out there wandering the streets alone?*

When the cops brought her, the girl had only been wearing a filthy, tattered dress that would probably disintegrate after a trip through the washing machine. No jacket, no shoes. That was okay. They'd get her some new clothes. And hopefully a new home to go with them.

"It's nice to meet you, Susan." Veronica leaned close and spoke in a confidential whisper. "And for the record, I don't like it when people use the short form of my name, either. I had a brother who called me Vee and it drove me bananas. I used to tell him Vee is a letter, not a name."

The girl said nothing; she stared at Veronica with an expression of mild interest.

"So why don't you tell me about yourself? Where do you live?"

The girl said nothing.

"Do you know where your parents are?"

Still nothing.

Veronica tried not to let her exasperation show on her face. Kids were magnets for negative feelings and she didn't want the girl to think she was upset with her. The kids who'd gone through hell weren't the ones you had to worry about. Plenty of kids who were abused went on to lead completely, or at least relatively, normal lives. The ones who required special care and attention were those who went to hell and never came back. The ones who turned inward and became completely unresponsive to the world around them. Dee Dee called them "kidatonic."

Veronica didn't think that was the case with this girl. Susan seemed able to carry on a normal conversation; she simply didn't feel like talking right now. She was frightened, maybe even in shock, but she'd come around eventually. Probably.

Fifteen minutes later, Veronica still wasn't able to get Susan talking again. The police arrived to pick her up. They had a place where she could get something to eat and a good night's sleep.

Veronica told Susan she'd see her again, even though it wasn't necessarily true. She had done the intake interview, but it didn't necessarily mean the girl's case would be assigned to her. She hoped it would be, though. There was something about the girl that touched her in a way she hadn't felt in a very long time.

It was too soon to tell if the girl had only passed through hell or taken up permanent residence, but Veronica had a good feeling about her. Maybe she could help her. Maybe she could turn that glow into a light bright enough to burn away all of the awful things that had been done to her.

Maybe.

"**Y**OU DID IT," Dee Dee said, "didn't you?"

"Did what?"

"Don't play dumb with me, girl. I'm way better at it than you."

Veronica picked up her gin-and-tonic and sipped it instead of replying. Which seemed to be answer enough for Dee Dee.

"I knew it," she said. "You got attached."

"What?"

"The kid. The girl. You let her in."

"I did not."

"I can see it." Dee Dee leaned forward, peering into Veronica's face. "You've got it. The twinkle."

Veronica flipped her the finger. "Twinkle on this!"

"I would if I wasn't a good Christian woman."

Veronica snorted. "You're not even a good woman."

"You got that right." Dee Dee slammed back the rest of her martini and signaled the bartender for another. "But I'm a damn fine drinking buddy."

Veronica raised her glass. "You're holding up admirably."

Dee Dee wobbled slightly on her stool, then steadied herself. "Getting attached," she said, shaking her head. "That's a rookie mistake. And since you're not a rookie — and haven't been for many, *many* years — you shouldn't be making a mistake like that."

Veronica lowered her head and nodded. She wouldn't have taken that kind of talk from anyone else, but her entire philosophy on child protection work had come from Dee Dee.

They'd both started at Brooklyn OCFS at the same time, almost twenty years ago. Veronica was from Brighton Beach, Dee Dee was from Red Hook. They had bonded over their names. When they first met, Dee Dee made the mistake of calling Veronica by the diminutive "Vee," and when Veronica expressed her contempt for the nickname, Dee Dee had responded, "Fair enough, girl. You don't call me Dee and I won't call you Vee. And if anyone refers to us as Vee-Dee, we'll make them wish their mothers never met their fathers."

Their friendship was bonded with that, and shortly thereafter came Dee Dee's philosophy, which amounted to this:

Lots of people worked in child protection services because they wanted to make a difference. Which was fine as long as they understood that "making a difference" didn't necessary mean taking children out of abusive homes and giving them better, happier lives. It was the ultimate goal, of course, and sometimes it actually happened, but anyone who thought they were playing on the winning team would do well to check the score board before they went running out onto the field.

Veronica didn't agree with this philosophy — not at first — but over time she came to learn exactly how difficult it was to remove a child from an abusive home. Between the rights of the parents and the bullshit bureaucracy of the system, it was a wonder any child was saved. Or as Dee Dee so eloquently put it: *You could catch the father sticking the kid with a pitchfork while the mother's high on blow and worshipping Satan in the next room, and you'd still be hard-pressed to convince a judge that the kid's better off in a foster home.*

The first two or three years had been rough for Veronica. If Dee Dee hadn't been there, she probably wouldn't have lasted. Eventually she came to accept the truth, that this was not a job that lent itself to optimism — in fact, it ate optimists for lunch. She might not have believed it if she hadn't seen it firsthand. Shiny new case workers who came in full of energy and enthusiasm, convinced they were going to swoop in like Spider-Man and save all the kiddies, only to realize the system worked against them rather than for them. She'd seen the way anger could lead to frustration, frustration to resentment, and if it wasn't checked quickly and firmly, those feelings could lead to drugs, or alcohol, or even suicide. Whatever it took to stop the pain and suffering leaking out of these poor, abused kids like radiation.

In the end, Dee Dee had helped her. Had saved her, if she was to be perfectly honest. Not by leveling with her or tempering her resolve. She'd merely put things into perspective: *It's not whether you win or lose, it's how you play the game.* Veronica didn't like the idea of comparing child protection work to competitive sports, but the words made sense. Because if you were going to last in this line of work, you had to understand it wasn't about keeping score. It wasn't about winning or losing. You did it because you had to try. It was the only thing that

mattered. Because doing nothing at all was worse.

The philosophy was soon followed by the motto, which Dee Dee told to Veronica on their first outing to Reggie's all those years ago. Gesturing with an empty martini glass for added emphasis, she'd said: *This is the most important thing you'll ever hear in your life. It should be painted in bright orange letters ten feet high on the wall of every children's aid office on the planet. You Can't Save Them All.*

It was a motto that became a way of life. Or at least a way to survive day to day. It also became their toast when they went out drinking after work.

"So," Dee Dee said, with a waft of vodka fumes that would've knocked over a plough horse. "What's the story on this latest urchin? The cops brought her in, right?"

Veronica nodded. "They found her wandering the streets in Bensonhurst. Completely non-responsive. No identification and none of the people in the area they questioned had any clue as to who she was or where she lived."

"A mystery," Dee Dee said.

"For now. Until she starts talking."

"You seemed to be doing all right in that department."

Veronica shrugged. "She clammed up pretty quick. And I don't even know if the cops are bringing her back."

"You sound disappointed. Remember what I said about getting attached?"

"I know. It's just..."

"This kid's different, right?" Dee Dee grinned. "You think I haven't said the same to myself a hundred times or more? Believe me, I've been there." She raised a hand to forestall Veronica's rebuttal. "And I'm not telling you to stay away. All I'm saying is be careful. The kid's fire, and fire can keep you warm, but if you get too close you can get burned."

"That might sound like wisdom if you weren't slurring your speech."

Dee Dee stared at her glass. "Liquor makes me

honest. And I don't want to see you get burned or get burned out. 'Cause then I'm out a drinking buddy. And without you I'm just an unwed forty-five-year-old with a drinking problem."

"You don't have a drinking problem, Dee Dee."

"I know, but if I didn't have you around to drink with, *that* would be a problem."

"More wisdom from drunk Yoda?"

Dee Dee gave Veronica a soft slap on the cheek. "Force is strong with you."

"The truth hurts, right?"

Dee Dee shrugged. "If it didn't, they wouldn't call it the truth."

THEY HUGGED OUTSIDE the bar, said they'd see each other tomorrow, and went off in separate directions.

Veronica huddled deep into her jacket. It was bitter cold and the wind had a sharp edge. *Another lovely January in New York*, she thought, and the image of the girl, Susan, came unbidden into her mind. Walking the frozen streets in her bare feet, her wisp of a dress the only thing between her emaciated body and the winter night.

She told herself to stop thinking about the girl. She told herself not to get attached.

You can't save them all.

It wasn't just a motto. It was advice. Damn good advice.

But if that were true, then why did she have such a hard time believing it?

Maybe she was getting weak. Maybe she *was* burning out.

Or maybe this girl was different. Maybe she was one of the few who could be saved.

She didn't know. She might never know.

She kept walking and tried to clear her mind.

But the thoughts remained, nipping at her like the cold nipped at her exposed skin. They followed her all the way home, and remained with her as she got ready for bed, following her down into sleep.

IT HAD BEEN a long time since she'd had the dream. It arrived like an unexpected guest, one she was neither happy nor surprised to see. The details were fresh and clear, like a memory of something that had happened yesterday instead of thirty years ago.

She saw the long wooden dock. She closed her dream eyes and heard the hollow thump of running footsteps on the plank boards. A moment of silence, followed by the splash.

Then the screams.

The cries.

"Help me, Vee! Help me, I can't..."

Veronica woke up gasping, as if she was the one screaming and crying. As if she was the one drowning.

As the dream dissolved, she sank back under blankets that were damp and rank with fear-sweat. She wished she still smoked, and wondered if there was a pack still hidden somewhere in the apartment, then decided she was too tired to look.

She didn't think about Trevor that much anymore. But she dreamed of him. Not often; at least not that she was aware of.

Trevor had died when they were kids. He didn't come from a troubled home, he wasn't abused or neglected or anything like that. He had simply fallen off the end of the dock at the family cottage and drowned in the lake. Their parents had forbidden them from going out on the dock without adult supervision. They had disobeyed this rule and Trevor had paid for it with his life. It was as simple as that. Or so Veronica told herself. But at night, the dream came, and there was nothing simple about it.

Someone with a rudimentary knowledge of psychology might have suggested Veronica had gone into child protection work because of her brother. Survival guilt and all that. And they would have been right. She could admit it, at least to herself if no one else. She'd never even told Dee Dee about Trevor.

She didn't know if she could explain the need to look out for kids the way she hadn't looked out for her brother. She knew it wouldn't bring him back, but it wasn't about that. She wasn't sure what it was about, but it didn't change the fact she was good at her job. And that was all that mattered.

She figured she wasn't the only person who got into this line of work on account of guilt or shame or some other form of emotional transference. If you really thought about it, those types of people probably made the best case workers. They were the only ones who could truly relate to the kids. The only ones who could really connect with them.

The way she had connected with Susan.

She wondered if she'd ever see the girl again. There had been something about her. She remembered the look the girl had given her, like maybe she had felt something, too. *You're different*, she had said.

"Well, you're different, too," Veronica told the empty room.

But that was okay.

Different was just another word for special.

"**S**HE'S BACK."

Veronica turned from her computer monitor to see Dee Dee standing in the entrance of her cubicle.

"What?"

"The prodigal waif. She hath returned."

"Susan?" Veronica said.

"That's the one. She's waiting for you in the reception area."

"Really?" Veronica was surprised. It had been a week since her brief meeting with the girl. Since the police never returned with her, Veronica had assumed the girl's parents, or another family member, had come to pick her up. Or that her case had been assigned to another office. She had been getting used to the idea she wouldn't see her again.

Dee Dee crossed her arms and leaned against the entryway. "Apparently the kid has been something less than cooperative with the police investigation."

Veronica leaned back in her chair. "Huh."

"I think it might be a federal thing," Dee Dee said.

"What makes you say that?"

Dee Dee shrugged. "The woman who brought her in looks like a fed. Expensive suit, bad shoes, attitude problem."

"She gave you attitude?"

"Not really," Dee Dee said. "But I could tell she was ready to if I gave her any shit. She's a redhead, and we all know gingers don't have souls. You piss them off at your peril."

"You're a redhead, Dee Dee."

"I'm the exception that proves the rule." A thin, amused grin touched her lips. "I got a vibe that Ms. Fed doesn't appreciate getting stuck with the babysitting detail. Her supervisor's probably some dumb male who thought sticking the kid with a female agent would help them bond or something. But I guess she doesn't have the nurturing instinct like we do."

"You think it's drug-related?"

"Possibly. Maybe Mummy and Daddy were busy cooking crystal meth and didn't notice the girl had wandered off. Or maybe they sniffed the authorities were closing in and decided to split sans child. Who knows? Nobody tells us shit, and that includes the girl." She heaved a big sigh. "If it *was* drugs it might explain why the kid isn't talking. Her parents may have told her to keep her mouth shut. We've seen it before — some of these kids, no matter how badly they've been treated, they'll hold burning coals in both hands if Mummy and Daddy tell them to. Either way, Ms. Fed — if that's what she is — thinks you might be able to get something out of the girl."

"Me?"

"I know, I'm surprised, too. Everyone knows I'm the best child whisperer in the office. But according to her, the kid only wants to talk to you."

"She said that?"

"Not in so many words." Dee Dee made a face. "Ms. Fed speaks almost as much as the kid."

❦

SUSAN WAS SITTING by herself in the reception area. Her head was down and she was gripping the sides of the chair while she swung her legs back and forth. She was alone. There was no sign of the redheaded federal agent.

Veronica said, "Hello there," and Susan looked up. "Do you remember me?"

Susan stared at her for a long moment, then said, "You're different."

"That's right," she said with a little laugh. "But all my friends call me Veronica."

"But not Vee," Susan said. "Vee is a letter, not a name."

"You got it." She was pleased the girl remembered her. "It's nice to see you again. You look a lot better than the last time I saw you."

It was true. Veronica almost didn't recognize her. She looked like a completely different girl. Her hair was clean, for one. It hung in a shimmering chestnut wave on either side of her face, which looked much less gaunt than it had before. She was wearing jeans and a sweater, both clean and new, and a winter jacket with a fur-lined hood. Veronica was relieved to see a pair of winter boots on her feet.

The only thing that hadn't changed were her eyes. The sockets weren't as dark and hollow, but she still had that blank far-off stare. As if she was looking through things rather than at them.

"How do you feel?" Veronica asked.

Susan shrugged and continued swinging her feet back and forth.

Veronica looked around. "I heard a woman dropped you off. Is she still around?"

"She said she'd be back later." Susan seemed to hesitate before adding: "I don't think she likes me." Another pause. "I don't think she likes anyone."

Veronica smiled. "Well, she's not here now."

"No, she's not," the girl observed.

Veronica held out her hand. "You want to get a bite to eat?"

❦

VERONICA TOOK HER to a diner she went to sometimes with the girls from the office. They sat in a corner booth, Veronica with a cup of coffee in front of her, Susan with a big piece of warmed-up apple pie, a blob of vanilla ice-cream melting on top of it. The girl hadn't touched it.

"So how have you been doing?" Veronica asked. "Are the police taking good care of you?"

Susan nodded.

Veronica wanted to ask about the woman who had dropped her off, if she really was a federal agent, but she didn't know if Susan would understand the question. Instead, she asked, "Have you heard from your parents?"

Susan said, "No parents."

"Your parents are gone?"

Susan shook her head.

"Are... did they pass away?"

Susan shook her head again. "No parents. Never had any."

Veronica frowned. What did that mean? Was she an orphan? Adopted? She supposed it might have meant either one of those things, but she had a feeling it didn't. There was something ominous and more than a little unsettling about the words she had used.

"I have a brother."

Veronica snapped out of her daze. "What? You have a brother?"

Susan nodded.

"Younger or older?"

She gave Veronica a funny look, like she didn't understand the question.

"Where is he?"

"Out there."

"Out where?"

Susan turned her head and stared out the window. Veronica followed her gaze. Beyond the glass she could see the parking lot, the snow-clogged street, and a line of streetlights glowing dimly against the winter evening.

"Out where?" she repeated.

"The house," Susan said. "He's waiting for me."

"What house?" Veronica said. "Your house?"

Susan shrugged.

"Where is it?"

Susan gave her that confused look again.

"Can you take me there?"

Susan nodded.

"Then let's go."

They went.

VERONICA DROVE BACK to Bensonhurst, where the police had originally picked up Susan. The girl didn't so much provide directions as point left or right as they approached certain intersections.

Eventually they ended up on a dark street of small brick houses that probably looked better for all the snow piled up around them. It wasn't so much a bad neighbourhood as it was a neglected one. Some of the houses only needed a coat of paint, while others would've benefited from a wrecking ball.

The house Susan directed her to was the worst-looking one on the street. Calling it a house was stretching things greatly. "Burnt-out ruin" would've been a more accurate description. The house had been two storeys at one time, but a fire had reduced it to one, with the remains of the second sitting atop the first like a blackened crown.

"This one?" Veronica said sceptically. "Are you sure?"

Susan nodded and climbed out of the car.

"Hey! Hold on a minute."

By the time Veronica undid her seatbelt and got out of the car, Susan was already across the snow-covered yard and climbing the porch steps.

"Don't go in there!" she yelled. "Wait for me!"

Susan either didn't hear her or didn't care. She pushed through the soot-stained front door hanging on a single hinge and disappeared into the house. Veronica ran after her, trying to dissuade images of the girl falling through the fire-damaged floor and plummeting into the basement.

But as she stepped across the threshold, she saw the house, at least the main floor, wasn't in bad shape. The walls were scorched and full of holes where the fire had chewed through, but the structure was mostly intact. A set of stairs climbing up to the non-existent second floor were blocked off at the top with sheets of plywood. The floor beneath her feet was soggy from wet snow or the water the firefighters had used to put out the blaze, but seemed strong enough to walk on.

"Susan! Where are you?"

She stood in what she guessed had been the living room. Through an archway, she saw Susan standing in the next room. She walked toward her with slow, careful steps, looking out for rusty nails or holes in the floor.

When Veronica reached Susan, she put a hand on the girl's shoulder, hoping to guide her out of the house and back to the car. There was something about this place she didn't like, something beyond the usual creepiness of an empty, abandoned house. But then she remembered why they had come here.

"I don't think your brother is here, Susan. I think maybe we should go now."

"He's here," Susan said. "He's been waiting for me."

"You've been gone a long time, honey. I think he might have left." Veronica made a show of looking around. "This isn't a very nice place. It's... dark."

Susan turned and looked at her. Her face was a pale oval with black holes for eyes. "We like dark places."

Then, as if someone had been waiting for the girl's signal, Veronica heard a board creak behind her. She spun around and saw a young boy walking slowly toward her. He was about Susan's age, wearing a pale button-down shirt and trousers with suspenders. All he needed was a flat cap and he would've looked like a newsie.

"Hi there," Veronica said. She was surprised to hear a tremble in her voice. "My name's Veronica."

"I know who you are," the boy said. He grinned. "You're different."

Veronica frowned. She had been amused when Susan had said that earlier. But now, in this place, from this boy, it bothered her.

"I told you," Susan said.

Veronica turned, thinking the girl was talking to her, but she was looking at the boy.

"She thinks I'm special."

The boy clapped his hands together and laughed. It was not a pleasant sound. Veronica detected a note of snide, almost condescending, amusement in it. As if she were the butt of a private joke between the two of them.

"She's outside," the boy said, "but she pretends she's not."

Susan abruptly cried out: "Help me, Vee! I'm drowning!"

Veronica felt the blood rush out of her face. Her mouth dropped open as she turned slowly to face the girl. In a small, barely audible voice, she said, "What did you say?"

But the reply came from the boy behind her: "Help me, please!"

Veronica snapped back around. She had to resist the urge to grab him by the upper arms and shake him.

"What is this?" she said. "What the hell is going on?"

"You're different," the boy said. His head was tilted to the side, as if he was studying her. "We're different, too."

That was an understatement, Veronica thought. She took a step toward a dark doorway she presumed led into the kitchen. She had to get away from these strange kids. She was starting to think she'd been played in some way she didn't understand.

"Can you read my mind?" she said, looking back and forth between them. "Is that it? Are you paramental?"

The girl let out a high-pitched shriek that Veronica supposed passed for a laugh in the language of spooky little kids.

"Is your name even Susan?"

The girl shrugged, as if her name, or any name, was meaningless to her.

Another thought, this one much more unpleasant than the idea of psychic children, rose in Veronica's mind.

"You're not human, are you."

It wasn't a question.

Which was fine, since neither the boy nor the girl chose to answer it.

"You're... monsters."

It sounded absurd coming out of her mouth, but she couldn't help it.

"Did you recognize us?" the boy asked, grinning.

"We're not the only monsters in this room," the girl said.

Veronica didn't say anything at first, but the girl's remark seemed to demand that she say something.

"I only see two," she said.

The girl smiled. "Oh, there's more than that!"

The sound of wood creaking and groaning suddenly rose up all around them. Veronica thought it was the house finally getting ready to collapse, but a second later she realized what it really was: the sound of small feet on the old, rotten floors.

Veronica looked all around as children poured into the room from both entrances. There were perhaps a dozen kids, boys and girls, all of them around the same age as Susan and her "brother," all of them dressed in old-fashioned clothing: dress shirts and vests and homespun gowns and blocky shoes. Not the sort of attire you'd find at Old Navy.

The children formed a ring around Veronica, staring up at her with gleaming eyes she could almost feel crawling on her skin. Susan stepped away from the others and reached out for her hand. Veronica recoiled, but not fast enough, and the girl's small hand closed around hers in a cold, powerful grip.

~

THE HOUSE WAS gone, but the sound of creaking wood was still there. So were the footsteps, but they were different — *You're different!* — they were faster, pounding the wooden floor, and she blinked and there was no floor, only a long dock stretching off into the shimmering blue water of the lake, and a boy shape getting small and smaller as it ran away from her.

It was Trevor, of course, her brother who'd drowned. An accident she at least partly owned. She was the one who had dared him to go to the end of the dock. Their parents forbade them to step even one foot on it if they weren't around, so the

ultimate dare was to go out to the very end of it. And after some prodding that escalated quickly to teasing, Trevor had gone off like a shot, not walking, not creeping, but sprinting down the dock, short legs pumping, shaggy hair flying. And it was here the film-reel of Veronica's memory experienced a sudden splice.

After the jump-cut, the sky turned darker, as if a cloud had passed in front of the sun, and Veronica was now running out toward the end of the dock.

Yes, she remembered this, of course she did, this moment haunted not only her memories but her dreams. The race to save Trevor. The race she never won.

Except Trevor wasn't in the water. He was standing at the end of the dock, smiling at her over his shoulder, his arms stretched out like Leo DiCaprio in *Titanic*. And years later when she saw that movie, she'd be reminded of this moment, and think *The little shit thought he was king of world, too.* Because this was what *really* happened. Trevor wasn't in the water when Veronica reached the end of the dock.

He didn't go in until Veronica pushed him.

She recalled the breathless gasp he made when her arms pistoned out and struck him, the way his body snapped with the recoil, the splash he made when he hit the water. It was so loud she thought her parents would come running. But they didn't. They'd polished off two bottles of wine with dinner the night before, and were still snoring away in the cabin.

Trevor popped up like cork, arms flailing, eyes wide with panic, and when he opened his mouth to call out for help, the lake poured in and he went back under. He came back up in a flash, spitting out some water, choking on the rest, and finally found his voice:

"Help me, Vee! I'm drowning!"

Veronica didn't move. She stood there with her arms crossed, a different Veronica, basking in the shadow-glow of a new dark day.

"My name isn't Vee."

🦟

"**H**E WAS THE first," Susan said.

"But not the last," the boy said.

Veronica blinked at them. She looked down and saw her arms were crossed. She didn't remember doing that. Apparently there were a lot of things she didn't remember doing. A lot of things she didn't notice. Like these kids. The two standing before her, and the others in a circle around her. Their eyes were black. Not like they had been abused. Their eyes were completely black. Empty, depthless voids.

She felt another void. She'd crossed her arms to hold it inside her, so she wouldn't fall into it. Except this void was more like a black hole. You didn't fall into it. It sucked you in with a powerful gravity. And when you were inside everything went dark for a while.

She could look into that darkness and see things. Things she had done. Bad things. She wasn't happy about them. She didn't feel anything about them, one way or the other. It was about putting things right, keeping the balance. Restoring order. And maintaining it.

She didn't do it often. That would have been foolish. She took one every two or three years. There was no reason behind it; something told her taking more would draw attention. Attention that could lead back to her. She was very careful, very discreet. And she became very good at it. It had taken time. Time and patience. And practice. Lots of practice. No one ever suspected her of anything, she was sure of it. Not even Dee Dee. How could they? If her parents had never suspected her about Trevor...

"He was the first," Veronica said. She nodded. It felt good to admit it. To speak the words aloud.

She looked at Susan and the boy, and the other kids, and for one horrible moment she thought these were the children she had taken, come back now to take her, like the karmic punchline in an episode of *The Twilight Zone*.

But no, these weren't her children. She knew their faces and these were not them. These black-eyed kids were monsters, not ghosts. So did that mean...

"We're not going to kill you," Susan said with a giggle. "We're going to take you away."

"Take me where?" Veronica asked.

Susan reached out and took her hand again. The boy took the other one. The other children broke their ring to let them pass through, and Susan and the boy led Veronica through the kitchen and outside.

The backyard was covered in a pristine blanket of white that seemed to pulse against the starless, moonless night. Susan and the boy drew her forward through the snow. She didn't know where they were taking her, and she didn't care. She closed her eyes and imagined she was walking along the dock at her family's cottage. She could see her brother standing at the end, his back to her, waiting. A cold gust of wind froze the smile on her face.

The snow was deep, but the kids didn't seem to have any trouble with it. She opened her eyes and saw their feet were standing on top of the crusted surface. She thought maybe they were ghosts, and squeezed their hands tighter. The kids squeezed back.

Susan said, "Are you ready, Vee?"

She nodded. The snow got deeper and the night got darker. She wanted to tell Susan that Vee wasn't a name, it was a letter, but she didn't care. There were worse things she could be.

She looked forward to all of them.

FICTION

THE NIGHT KINGDOM

Shikhar Dixit

SEE, THIS GUY, let's call him Bob, his girl had just left him, and he'd just gotten fired from UPS after 25 years with the company. I mean, how do you like that? 25 years, and no severance package — "

"I thought you said this was a ghost story."

"First of all, I said 'spooky story.' There's no ghost in it, but there is — well, look, if you would just shut up and listen, I'll get to it!"

"All right," I said. "Go on." I sipped my lager, looked around the bar. Clientele was solid working class, just the way I liked it. This was where the real stories were.

"Thank you! All right, so he's jobless and his lady's kicked him out. So he packs up his stuff and finds a crappy little place in New Brunswick, see? Real dump. So he's in this apartment, unpacking, and he finds this book. And it's really strange, because he's not a big reader, y'know? He's only got maps and an old cook book that used to be his ma's. But here's this book."

McCantyre, who goes by Mac, a largish man of muscular build, gone slightly to seed, leans in, blocking the light, "He calls it a black bible, but it ain't no bible and it ain't black. It's red cloth and it has only three words on the cover."

"The Night Kingdom"

I sat up, interested now. *The Night Kingdom?* I wasn't sure why, but the name made the hair stand up on the back of my neck.

"So he reads the book, of course, just sittin' there on the floor, and the light comin' through the window gets dimmer as it gets later, and he learns some things — things maybe a person shouldn't know, know what I mean?"

"Where did you get this from, again?"

Ignoring me, Mac continued, "After that, he changes. In a big way, get me? He stops lookin' for work. He lets himself go. Ain't eatin' too well, anyway, what with the old bank account shrinking. No exercise. Stops calling his brother. And he starts spendin' his savings on odd books. This guy, the non-reader, and suddenly he can't have enough books. But we're not talkin' James-friggin-Patterson here. No Stephen King for Bob. Real arcane shit — expensive.

"His brother thinks he's cracked like a hot chestnut, what with losing the girl and the job in the same week. Tries to get him committed."

Mac gulped his Budweiser. To me, this is a poor choice when someone offers to buy you a drink, but Mac stated proudly that he was a "Bud man through and through." I took another sip of my own drink.

"There's a big back-and-forth over Bob's mental fitness. They put him in some institution for observation an' shit. Bob freaks out in that place, sayin' how he needs his books. That — here it gets a little funny, and not in a happy way, know what I'm sayin' — he needs to 'Say the rituals before each sunrise,' or somethin' bad will happen to him. He tells his psychiatrist that he'll kill his wife for him, that he knows the doc wants to, if they'll just give him his precious books.

"Man, it just gets more fucked after that. The doctor tries to strangle Bob, right there in his office — "

"You're making this up — "

"No, I'm not! I'm not. That doctor, the psychiatrist, he's the top dude at this place. Hans Werthaim. His personal secretary's my sister. This is for real!"

We both paused here, pulling at our drinks, eyeing each other in some kind of contest. Mac looked away first, but I felt it in my gut; this was the real deal. He wasn't lying.

"So what happens after that?"

"The doctor goes on leave, a nice long rest — for his nerves, they say. My sister says that just means they're trying to cool things off, avoid a scandal."

"Sounds about right to me. What about Bob?"

"Locked up. The brother signs the papers. End of story." Mac sucked down the last of his beer.

"But what about the book?"

Mac just shrugged.

I SHOULD HAVE left it alone. I know that now.

But at the time, I thought it was a chilling tale. I got what I came for, a lead for a new story. I was a reporter for the Glyph Herald. In my defense, I'm pretty sure now that something else was pulling the strings, that my fate was more or less sealed the moment Mac finished his story.

Oh, and something else I was able to ascertain even before I'd started: Dr. Hans Werthaim's personal secretary is a man.

A GREAT DEAL of research and digging revealed that the "Bob" in question was, in fact, Eric Robert Sandoval, formerly a delivery driver for UPS. Presently, he was safely locked away in St. Dymphna's Psychiatric Hospital, a private institution in upstate New York. There was little chance I'd be allowed to speak to him, so I instead sought out and found his brother and last living relative, John Sandoval, ensconced in an affluent suburb of Glyph. The town in which I grew up and to which I returned after college

I was able to walk to his house from the bus station. I knocked on his door this fine Saturday afternoon without a clue as to what I would say when he opened up. As it turned out, the door was already open. I rapped on the door frame and called out, "Hello!"

There was no answer. I stood on the threshold of a darkened room, thick with shadows and absent of any signs that it had ever been inhabited by the living. "Hello!" Nothing.

I stepped into the room, a fairly large one, whose huge bay window was covered over with thick layers of newspaper. The deeper shadows were abuzz with flies, their ceaseless drone making me uneasy.

The large room led through beaded curtains into an even darker corridor. Here, I detected the sound of more flies as well as an unpleasant odor I associated with spoiled milk. I stood in a small kitchen with an attached dining nook. A round table with three rickety-looking chairs stood in the nook. On its surface, which was layered with newspapers, was an object covered with flies. I thought, later on, that it might have been someone's tongue. The spoiled milk odor gave way here to the definite stench of decomposition. I felt suddenly dizzy with revulsion and a surging terror.

I turned away from this and stood debating whether to continue searching or to abandon the house and, perhaps, call the police. After a moment, I turned right and went through another short hall into a small living room. A large flat-screen TV and entertainment center stood collecting dust. All the windows here were also papered over.

Just beyond this room's other entrance, I found stairs ascending to the second floor. I climbed with growing trepidation. The rotten smell was rising again as I reached the landing. Only the dimmest of light penetrated from the three bedrooms I could see from the head of the stairs.

The first two rooms were empty save the homey-looking child-sized beds and furniture. One seemed fitted out for a boy, the other for a girl. I didn't linger in either one of these; I moved down the hall, past the stairs, to what I guessed would be the master bedroom.

The smell was strong enough here that I felt bile rise up from the back of my throat. For the first time since beginning this venture, my head seemed to grow clear enough for me to consider leaving the premises. Was I truly interested in seeing what lay beyond this door?

A sharp, wooden rapping sound issued from within the room.

Taking a deep breath, I pushed the door open. It was a master bedroom, as I'd thought, and along the right-side wall was a short hall, probably leading to a bathroom and walk-in closet. Nearer than that, however, a queen-size bed drew my attention. I felt all of the breath halt in my lungs. The odor was definitely from decomposition. I slapped my hand over my mouth and nose, a part of me wanting to cover my eyes with the other one.

The sheets might once have been white or off-white; it was difficult to tell in the dimness. In the yellowish cast of light leaking through both the lacy white drapes and newspaper-covered windows, the entire bed seemed to be stained black. Amidst a tangle of sheets lay three bodies, or rather, portions of bodies, wrapped in places while exposed in others. The ragged edges of wounds and severed limbs looked especially cruel in the semi-darkness. I felt paralyzed by the sheer brutality of the scene. Two of the bodies were on the small side, probably children. Air started to move through my windpipe again, a heaving sigh and hitch which I didn't immediately realize was the sound of me crying. The odor of death didn't seem quite so important anymore.

That hollow clack resounded again, from beyond the short hallway. It reminded me of the sound those scene boards made when smacked closed before a camera, the kind of raw footage you only found in the "Special Features" on blu-rays unless you worked in the film industry. The sound repeated itself, a great deal louder, and I feared, also closer. Something shifted amidst the deep shadows of the little hallway where the bathroom might be. From my angle, only a small portion of it was visible, something large and round that stuttered and jerked like a marionette, but with changeable momentum, like a video running at double speed, then dropping back to real-time.

I was overcome by primal terror as something massive emerged into the room proper, something that clacked with what I could only consider to be an air of menace.

Then I turned and fled, around the corner and down the stairs. I careened around corners and only drew to a halt when I came into the large front room, for sitting on a coffee table before the great window was a small book. The glint of foil-stamping caught my attention now that I had grown used to the dimness. That is what I told myself, then.

I snatched it up and barged out the front door. Shoving the little hardback into my jacket pocket, I jogged nearly all the way to the bus stop.

☃

ON THE BUS, I shook with a queasy kind of horror. I had entered a crime scene — trespassed, actually, just walked right on into somebody's house. Where might I have inadvertently laid my hand? Were my fingerprints on the table in the large room, in the kitchen, just waiting to be collected by some crime scene tech? Had I touched the door jamb as I stood on the threshold of that bedroom, just a few feet away from three human bodies? My heart was trip-hammering and my t-shirt was sodden with perspiration.

And then there was the other thing — the creature I had come to think of as "The Puppet." What had motivated that particular hallucination? Or was I coddling myself? Was there really an otherworldly, demonic presence in John Sandoval's bedroom?

I toyed, ever so briefly, with the thought of calling the police, confessing my presence and my purpose, and immediately tossed that idea aside. There was no reason for my prints or DNA to be in any database. It was highly unlikely that authorities would ever cross my path, or I theirs, regarding the murders (they almost certainly had to have been murdered) of the Sandoval family.

When I got into my apartment, I pulled off my jacket. The pocket swung heavily and bounced off my elbow. I had completely forgotten about the book.

I pulled it out with trepidation. If I had been expecting the book from Mac's story, *The Night Kingdom* (and I was, wasn't I?), I was disappointed. It was dark brown and vinyl-covered, not red. The word "Journal" was embossed in cheap, flaky gold-coloured paint across the front cover.

I dropped it on the table in the living room, went into the kitchen to get a beer, paused to reconsider, and grabbed a clean glass and bottle of Jim Beam from the cabinet instead.

After pouring myself three-fingers' worth, I sat down in the living room, took the journal into my hands, and opened it. The fly-leaf had the words "Property of J. Sandoval" scratched out in a neat, spiky cursive, and below, in the same hand, but a different ink, "If found, please mail to," followed by

Sandoval's Glyph address.

I turned to the next page and the first entry was there, dated "March 4th, 2012." Though the handwriting was lovely, John Sandoval's very best Palmer-method script, the quality of his prose left a bit to be desired. And the content, day-after-day of utterly mundane, insignificant details, made for a difficult read. I persisted.

Nearly an hour passed, me turning the pages, sipping occasionally from my glass. At one point, I stopped and felt an abrupt lump of dread, as I realized that I could add theft and tampering with evidence to my already long list of crimes for the day. I finished my whiskey in one gulp and refilled my glass.

About halfway through the journal, after faithfully writing every day, Sandoval apparently didn't write for an entire week. The dates, which jumped from May 6th to May 13th, also marked a noticeable change in his formerly precise and copious hand. What remained after this pause I have copied out verbatim:

MAY 13 - Eric's problem might be contageaous (sic). Have noticed odd things around the house since taking him up to Dymphna's. Seeing shadows where there shouldn't be, hearing noises, like someone writing on a blackboard back in the day.

Here, there was a two-line break, also unusual in this journal, as Sandoval was very economical concerning writing space, letters small and close together, with never a single space between entries.

Got to get over to Eric's apt. and gather things tomorrow. Don't know what to do with his crazy col. of books.

Here, another three days were missed.

MAY 17 - Spoke to Mackenzie on phone today. Says Eric had (illegible) last month. This was news to me. I pressed him, but he would only say to forget about it. Throw away the book, he says. I say I can't just throw out a thousand dollars' worth of books. He says something strange like, you only got to get rid of the one. What one? Sonofabitch tells me not to call again and hangs up. This from Eric's best friend, the son of a bitch!

Or course, I wondered if this Mackenzie was the very same "Mac" who told me about Eric, or rather "Bob", in the first place. The unreadable word was so indecipherable that I could not even conjecture what it might have been.

MAY 19 - Jordan and Racquel were scared when I got home today. Babysitter also seemed shaken, but said everything was fine. I can't get them to tell me anything specific. Just say that the dark parts of the room got bigger. Can't figur (sic) what that means.

MAY 23 - I know what book, now. Have read it and wish it could be unread. The Black Book, Eric called it, but it is red not black. The Night Kingdom. God help me God help us the book is not just a book at all. I FEEL COMPELLED!

Originally, there were two Gods. Jehovah, the Lord Of Hosts, and an Anti-God! This Dark Anti-God created servants with "a deep and abiding hunger." When Jehovah sealed away "the First Darkness" in "The Night Kingdom," these servants were left behind and "their very filaments severed." Like puppets. But the cutting of their strings gave the puppets free will. But certain steps needed and I FEEL COMPELLED to complete them. Damn you, Mackenzie, I know this started with you and I'm going to kill you before it takes me.

I was deeply shaken by these words, and would have thrown away the journal right there and then, but I noticed that there was only one more entry, on the very next page.

MAY 27 - Mackenzie is out of reach. Eric is out of reach. The front porch is out of reach. Hail Mary, Full of Grace, The Lord is with thee. Blessed art thou among women, and blessed is the fruit of thy womb, Jesus. Holy (unreadable) it doesn't matter, they are close. I've put Jordan and Racquel down they are safe with their mother but I will never be safe never be safe again God forgive me Jesus forgive me. No more words. Words can't fix it. I already miss them but they're with Shailene now. Enough. Goodbye.

That was all. The writing had deteriorated badly at

the end, and so too, I think, had John Sandoval. But that bit about two gods — it sounded familiar. I put down the journal, pulled my iPhone from my pocket, and tapped open the browser. Less than five minutes of searching, and I found this:

"[T]he Christians of Languedoc
The *Cathars*, who were *Dualists*, believed in two principles, a good God and his evil adversary, *who was not Satan*, but rather, another god. The good *God* was the Lord of the *New Testament*, the creator of the spirit world. The evil god, the god whom no one worships, is the lord of physicality. He created all visible matter in the universe, including the human body..."

Apparently, amongst the Cathars, there existed an elite, an aristocratic class entrusted with "secret knowledge." As with the Ancient Greek Mystery cults, they were ceremonially sworn to protect this knowledge. But *what* secret knowledge? There was nothing about puppet servants with "a deep and abiding hunger." No antithesis to the hierarchies of God's angels. But then, those might be the Mysteries of the elect.

Pouring myself another glass nearly to the brim, I drank it down in relatively few gulps. The day had been long and the night would be longer, I was sure. Tomorrow, I would call out of work and then burn the journal with charcoal and lighter-fluid in my old-school circular barbecue grill until nothing but ashes remained. What was left of my curiosity after the Sandoval house was well and truly spent.

ONE BIG QUESTION remained, however. Having merely discovered (stolen) the private journal of John Sandoval, where was the promised black bible? Did *The Night Kingdom* even exist, or was Mac tale-spinning? On the tail of that thought, another slipped into my head before I could avoid it. What if Mac was an agent of an old religion? A member of the modern-day "elect," well versed in the Mysteries. The Mysteries of The Night Kingdom. But I'd asked that big question only to myself. Whoever Mac was, he was an agent of no good. I just wanted out.

Of course, it was too late for that.

I AWOKE IN my bed around 3am.

There was a clatter upon the roof and against my nearest window, accompanied by a sudden blast of thunder that nearly stopped my heart.

I got myself up, still in the same clothes I wore in John Sandoval's house. I approached the window, which I had covered with dense, dark curtains; it kept the morning light out since I worked nearly graveyard shift hours, producing my best writing in earliest morning.

When I shifted the curtains, I found a scene completely unfamiliar. No backyards or fencing. Just endless fields as far as my sight allowed.

The noisy clatter, I had ascribed to sleet or hail. Neither was the culprit.

It was a rain of human teeth. They were collecting in a small heap along the outer track of my horizontally sliding window. Most had bloody roots, residual meat from when they'd been cruelly pulled from their gums.

All the fine hairs along the back of my neck and upon my forearms were standing up. My heart seemed to stutter from revulsion and horror. A low-grade nausea gripped me, but I could not look away. My small, square house no longer appeared to be in Glyph.

It would soon be buried under several inches of molars, incisors, canines, bicuspids, etc, pulled during ritual torture. How I knew this I couldn't begin to fathom. But I knew.

MY ATTEMPTS TO use the phone were met with silence. No dial tone on my landline. No connection on my cell. There appeared to be no internet connection, despite my high-speed set-up. Similarly, my phone could not send or receive text messages.

When human reality becomes a nightmare, escape into sleep can seem a pleasant dream. I laid in bed for 1 to 2 days; each time I awoke, for just a few precious moments I thought it had all been a bad dream. But the sound of raining teeth would eventually penetrate my nice dream and return me to reality. And so I would retreat once more into sleep.

One day I woke up and immediately noticed the golden stripe. When last I'd looked out of the window, I'd left the curtains open just 2 or 3 inches. My bedsheets are a uniform beige, and when I looked down and saw the golden stripe of light from beyond the curtains, the idea that at least some of the last two days had been a nightmare became plausible.

Climbing out of bed with sudden urgency, I crossed the room, opened the curtains, and checked the window tracks outside. Spiders, yes, but teeth? Not a trace. I saw my overgrown backyard and my collapsing fence and started to cry. Better still, I saw that my backyard abutted another backyard belonging to the house on the next street. An annoying man and his loud, aggressive dog lived there. And if I met him at the fence line today, I would apologize for my past complaints and set about becoming his friend.

I GOT MY cheap, very old grill burning. The lighter fluid nearly cost me my eyebrows. The first thing to go into the flames was John Sandoval's private journal. My handwritten notes from my conversation with Mac followed. It took a while, but just then my grasp on concepts such as time had rather loosened. I stood over it as long as nobody came outside into one of the adjacent yards. I was still there long after the fire had gone out. Finally, out of sheer boredom, I went inside.

A genuinely warm feeling suffused me; I felt that I'd been granted a second chance. I'd been spared and given the opportunity to avoid making the same error in the future.

Then I turned toward my work area, my enormous, teak writing desk, and there lay a red cloth-bound hardcover book, lacking only a dust-jacket. On the front cover, stamped in gold, three words: *The Night Kingdom.*

My first thought was to grab it and throw it on the grill, and add lighter fluid. Some feeling in me rebelled. I decided that I did not want to touch that book; I definitely didn't want to read it. I headed toward the door. The hallway outside my bedroom, usually filled with daylight, was packed with massive, shifting shadows.

CLACK!

My stomach lurched. My heartbeat accelerated. A moment later, a distinct CLACK resounded down the short, low-ceilinged hallway. A heavy darkness consumed the restless points of light. An ungainly silhouette, a being designed to be controlled from above, jittered just beyond the threshold. Granted self-determination, it would forever struggle for balance. I doubted that such a creature could ever be destroyed by man.

Something occurred to me; several characters from the Bible had visitations from angels. The seraphim, whose celestial beauty was occasionally remarked upon in even later books of the apocrypha, were numerously depicted in Renaissance art and by the Pre-Raphaelites. This being, on the other hand, possessed long straight limbs, covered in loose wattles of skin, fair as sycamore bark. Its slightly cylindrical head abruptly bisected horizontally, revealing two curved lips of some lethally sharp substance, which caused me to flinch as it clacked them shut. I sensed that it knew the depths of my terror. Raising its monstrously long, rigid arm, it pointed a long blade of a finger at The Night Kingdom. I backed away until the book was within my reach and opened to the first page, where English words in small print marched across the surface.

The volume was densely packed with hundreds and hundreds of the dark god's commandments.

Taking up the book in my shaking hands, I began to read. I read for several hours. As night fell outside, I stopped reading and looked up. The dark god's servant still stood there, blocking the exit from my bedroom. Exhausted, my hands sore from grasping Mac's black bible, I kept reading.

I READ UNTIL dawn. It shouldn't have been possible, with all I'd been through, but for the unholy power of that other God — the one who led me here, to an understanding of the flesh that few living men or women possessed. If one possessed physicality, rather than just pure spirit, one could be enslaved by the Anti-God.

After all that reading, the manacles that locked me into service were my own body and brain.

John Sandoval managed to escape. I didn't.

My next instruction was to find and kill Dr. Hans Werthaim. No reason was given to me. But I already knew why ... that murder would presage the return of another God. A darker God whom Yahweh once successfully tricked before time began. This journal I have left for the next opener of the way. Even in this, I was only carrying forth His wish. The new God is not a believer in free will.

There is no longer any choice at all.

DIM SHORES PRESENTS
VOLUME 2 / WINTER 2020

NEW STORIES FROM

Mike Adamson / Randee Dawn / J.W. Donley
Timothy G. Huguenin / Jennifer Loring / Avery Kit Malone
C.M. Muller / Mari Ness / dave ring / Erica Ruppert
Michael David Wilson / Jake Wyckoff

DIM SHORES PRESENTS is a bi-annual anthology series spotlighting some of the best new writing in speculative fiction. Weird horror, strange science fiction, and dark fantasy rub shoulders with each other here, weaving a tapestry of uncanny beauty and fearful wonder. For more information or to sign up for the mailing list, please visit dimshores.com.

DIM SHORES

Post Office Box 3092
Citrus Heights, CA
95611-3092, USA
DIMSHORES.COM

FICTION

WHERE THE HOLLOW TREE WAITS

John Langan

MARTIN'S FATHER was waiting for him when he came down to start the coffee maker.

It was painfully early, the kitchen windows still dark, but the Mr. Coffee had reached the point where, no matter how much vinegar Martin ran through it to keep it clean, it required a good forty-five minutes to brew the six cups of coffee. Time to invest in a new coffee maker, obviously, though funnily enough, they had bought a shiny black model (some German brand) at Wal-Mart six or maybe eight months ago (the trip was among the last he had taken with Cassie), only to have it stop working altogether one morning, thus necessitating a return to the lethargic Mr. Coffee. At some point, Martin would return to Wal-Mart, or possibly Target,

for another, sturdier replacement; in the meantime, he set the alarm on his tablet for an hour he hated to see twice in a day and lumbered down the protesting staircase to ensure there would be coffee waiting for his son's awakening. Seventeen, Fred required a series of jolly threats to rouse him in time to be ready for the school bus, and the reward of a mug of coffee, light and sweet, once he had emerged from his bedroom with its fish tanks and their bubbling filters.

From behind their pebbled plastic shield, the fluorescents revealed Les, Martin's father, sitting crosswise in a chair on the opposite side of the kitchen table, his left arm resting on the back of the chair, his right on the table. He was dressed, the denim jacket he favoured over one of the plaid shirts he also preferred. His thick hair, the color of steel, had been brushed into a rough pompadour. Mouth closed, his lower jaw moved side to side, as if he were worrying at something caught in his teeth. His watery blue eyes stared at nothing, visualizing, perhaps, the topography of his mouth; nonetheless, he nodded as Martin entered the kitchen. Martin did not return the greeting. After clicking the switch that brought the coffee maker to stuttering life, he poured himself a glass of water from the tap, set it aside, and reached for the orange plastic pill bottle on the shelf to his left. The chunky Metformin tablet he took for his diabetes tasted slightly sweet as it lay on his tongue waiting for the water to wash it down, which never failed to strike him as...funny? Ironic? Which never failed to strike him, anyway. Without turning around, he finished the water and set the cup on the counter.

"You know," he said. Sleep had thickened his voice into an old man's croak. He cleared his throat, tried again. "You know, I had a dream about you last night." He glanced over his shoulder, saw his father had shifted in his chair to sit face-forward, both elbows on the table. From this angle, the old damage to Les's face was unavoidable, his flattened nose, the scars radiating from it like grooves in leather cracked and worn.

"We were out in front of the house," Martin continued. "You, me, Fred, Cassie," at his wife's name, Martin's voice quavered, "and Susan and Deirdre. I don't know if you met them. They were friends of Fred's. Susan was in his grade; Deirdre was her younger sister — is her younger sister. We've known the family since Fred and Susan were in preschool together. Their parents worked late, so the girls used to come here for a couple of hours after school. Cassie and I called them our surrogate daughters." The memory raised a brief smile. "They stopped coming once Susan hit middle school and declared herself capable of looking after the two of them by herself. Their parents agreed. We still see them once in a while. Their family comes over here for dinner; we

— Fred and I — go to their house for dinner.

"In my dream, the girls were here and they were young, the way they'd been when we watched them. So was Fred — although he was a couple of years older, late middle school/early high school. When I dream about him, he's usually that age. Doesn't take much of a psychologist to explain why, I suppose. The three kids were playing, running around the lawn, too close to the road for my comfort, but there were no cars around. I was standing nearer to the house, in line with the picture window in the living room. On my right, Cassie was at the front door. I could just see her from the corner of my eye. I wanted to look at her directly, but I was afraid I'd find her gone...and more afraid I'd find her there." Martin licked his lips. "She was speaking, her voice low. I had trouble understanding her words. You — as I said, you were there, too. You were standing on the little mound in the middle of the lawn, where the cedar used to be, the one we had to cut down after it died and we became concerned about it falling on the house. Although you were facing me, your eyes were focused on the ground. You were doing your best to give the impression you weren't paying attention to anything around you, but you never were much good at that kind of deception. It was clear you were aware of everything."

The Mr. Coffee burped, hissed, sighed, releasing a wisp of steam from the gap between its top and the filter basket. A shuffle step to his left, the sole of his foot scraping the unswept floor, allowed Martin a clearer view of the knife block next to the coffee maker, while another check over his shoulder showed Les moved to one end of the table, where he had again positioned himself sideways in his chair.

"One of the girls," Martin said, "Deirdre, the younger one, stopped playing. She'd noticed something in the woods across the street. In the impulsive, reckless way kids have, she dashed onto the road. I yelled at her to stop, but she was already in the trees. The woods aren't very deep. They run parallel to the entire street, but they go back only a hundred yards or so before a drop off to the highway. We've seen deer scat over there, what I was sure was a heap of bear shit one time, which Cassie and Fred thought was the funniest thing, wouldn't stop teasing me about...The point is, I wasn't as worried about Deirdre running into any wild animals as I was her reaching the drop and falling into the path of an eighteen-wheeler. Susan was starting to follow her sister, Fred to follow her. I shouted for them to stay where they were. Between my weight and my knees, running isn't my strong suit. I was waiting for someone to chase after Deirdre, either Cassie or you, but never once did your expression change, despite my yelling. I had no doubt you knew what was happening and were amused by it. Or not amused, exactly: the emotion you were radiating was...darker. I was distressed enough to turn to Cassie, only to find the space at the front door empty. My heart contracted, but there wasn't time for grief right then. Deirdre was in the trees. There was no other option except for me to start after her.

"Even in my unconscious, I don't run especially fast. Reaching the other side of the street seemed to take hours, and along the way, every detail stood out to me with hallucinatory clarity, from the lawn whose grass was yellowed and brittle from lack of rain, to the road, whose surface was covered by old stains like a psychiatrist's inkblots, to the tall grass lining the other side of the street, whose stalks had been matted down in places by whatever animals had slept there. Beyond the grass, the trees stood in loose ranks, maples, mostly, their leaves dull with dust. I ducked under their branches and was in a vast dim space, the trunks of the maples and a few, scattered pines rising up like the columns of a temple, someplace ancient, their crowns forming the roof fifty or sixty feet above. Of Deirdre, there was no sign. I called her name, thought I heard her laughing somewhere farther into the woods. Thinking of the drop off, I ran toward the sound of her laughter."

Its rich, heavy odor filling the kitchen, coffee trickled into the pot, the Mr. Coffee laboring away. Martin shifted another half-step left, resting both hands palms-down on the counter's cool Formica, the fingertips of his left hand inches from the black handles of the knives slotted into the knife block's blond wood. His latest look at Les revealed him sitting sideways in one of the chairs on the near side of the table. Martin thought his father's eyes had regained some of their focus, possibly all, but between the way Les had positioned himself and the angle from which

Martin was spying him, it was difficult to say for sure. One thing of which there was no doubt, however, was Les's utter concentration on the words Martin was stitching together; he could feel his father's attention as if it were a third person in the room with them, one furtive and malevolent. Martin let his fingers slide closer to the knife block.

"You know how it is in dreams," he said. "Familiar places are strange, often dramatically so, to the point the sole reason you know where you are is because something within the dream has told you so. The ground was bare of leaves and needles, as if it had been swept clean. Dark blotches discoloured the trees' bark. A fungus, I assumed, though the patches kept threatening to turn into faces. I did my best not to look at them too closely, but I had the sense they were not returning the courtesy. The flesh on my arms and legs crawled. Rose and gold light streamed into the space from directly in front of me, the setting sun putting on its final show for the day. I ran in that direction, stopping every few paces to shout Deirdre's name, but there was no more answering laughter. Vines wrapped the trunks of the trees I struggled past, their leaves shining with the sun's dying light, and something about the vines, a certain regularity — neatness, even — made me think they had been wound around the trees, as opposed to having grown there normally. The setting sun reduced the rows of trunks ahead to black silhouettes. Squinting against the glare wasn't enough. I raised my hand to shield my eyes. Dark forms wavered in the light in a way that caused my mouth to dry, my throat to tighten. I had the distinct impression any one of them might take a step toward me on legs too long, legs monstrously long. All of it, the entire wood, seemed on the verge of erupting into furious movement.

"A great, deafening sound shook the trees, as if someone had played a chord on the world's largest pipe organ. I flinched, sure this was the signal for everything to move on me. Then the sun dipped below the horizon, the rose-gold light eased to a dimmer, blue-tinted glow, and I could see a clearing before me. The trees surrounding it were different — I want to say they were simpler, which doesn't make any sense, I know. Each consisted of a slender trunk and a dense crown of leaves, like a quick sketch of a tree. They weren't as tall as the maples and pines, maybe fifteen feet, twenty at the most. At the center of the clearing, a single, dead tree tilted to my right. In life, it would have been enormous, a king of the forest. About ten feet up, it had snapped; there was no sign of the rest of it. Its leaves, branches, bark had been stripped away; the wood was gray. Even so diminished, it was...vast. A deep channel ran up it from bottom to top, as if generations of woodpeckers had drilled away its heart. Within that dark seam, I saw movement and realized a person was trapped in there, deep inside. How this had happened, I couldn't say, but at the moment, I wasn't particularly concerned. I had found Deirdre. I called to her, told her not to worry, I was here, and ran across the clearing.

"As I approached the tree, I saw that both sides of the groove were smeared with blood, the entire length of the trunk. In the fading light, it appeared more black than red. There was no way, I thought, anyone could lose this much blood and survive. I said Deirdre's name, but there was no reply. My pulse was pounding in my throat, my chest hollow with dread. The gap in the tree went farther than I had realized, to the point it seemed to extend right to the other side of the trunk. This close, the smell of the blood was overwhelming. My dread was breaking down into anguish, confusion, when I saw the figure inside the tree, way back within that wood chasm. It wasn't Deirdre. This person was bigger, older, an adult. Her hair was long, thick, tangled with twigs and dead leaves. She was wearing a slip whose white satin was smudged and stained with earth and blood. The skin of her arms and legs was crisscrossed with scratches, a few deepening into cuts. She was wedged into the tree, so tightly I couldn't believe she could be alive, but her head swung toward the sound of my voice.

"It was Cassie," Martin said. "I knew — I had known it was her the instant I saw her stuck in there. She lifted her right arm, reached to me. Right away, I was pressed against the tree, left hand braced against the wood as I stretched as far into the gap as I could with my right. The blood along the seam's edges lacquered the side of my face, my shirt, but I didn't care. I was frantic to touch the tips of Cassie's fingers, to grab them, to seize her palm, her wrist, to pull her out of here, bring her back to me. I couldn't, though. No matter how hard I squeezed myself into the opening — and I could feel the wood bruising and breaking my skin — our hands remained hopelessly far apart. I was crying, sobbing. Cassie was talking to me, all the while moving further into the tree, as if it was slowly swallowing her. 'Your father,' she said. 'He never came back from that last hunting trip. I'm so sorry,' she said, which was insane, her apologizing to me. 'I'm so sorry, he's — ' But I couldn't understand what she said next. 'Earl,' or, 'Url' something."

Martin shook his head. "That was all of it. I woke — had cried myself awake, actually. I wasn't much inclined to return to sleep, and then the alarm went off, so I made my way down here. Where I found you, as I have every morning since Cassie — for the last month and a half." The slightest turn of his head showed Les (the Earl Croning?) standing behind him. His mouth was open in a wide grin. Instead of the crooked mess of his teeth, his gums were thickets of splinters and twigs, picket lines thick with amber sap. The same syrupy liquid spread over Les's eyes. From within the broken wood in his mouth, the creak of a tall tree, a king of the forest moving in a strong wind, issued forth. "She was gone a month before they found her," Martin said, his left hand closing on the molded plastic of the carving knife's handle. "They wouldn't tell me everything that had happened to her, said they couldn't be sure. You know, though, don't you?" The creak grew louder, as if the great tree were preparing to crash on him.

Two things happened. Fred's door opened, and Martin yanked the knife from the block, pivoting to sweep its serrated edge in an arc bisecting the space where Les (*the Url Groaning?*) was standing.

"Um, Dad?" Fred said, padding into the kitchen, the drowsiness on his features fleeing at the sight of Martin standing back to the counter, the carving knife ready in his left hand, his chest heaving, his face flushed. Fred paused next to the refrigerator. "Is everything okay? I thought I heard you talking to someone. That's why I got up."

"So that's what it takes," Martin said, turning to replace the knife shakily in its slot. With hand not much steadier, he opened the cabinet in front of him and retrieved Fred's favorite mug.

"I'm serious," Fred said, all of his adolescent earnestness on display. "I couldn't hear what you were saying, but it sounded pretty intense. Are you all right?" Under the surface of his question, Martin heard a plea: "Please tell me I'm not about to lose you, too."

Martin poured his son a cup of coffee, handed it to him to add milk and sugar to.

"Well," he said.

"Siehst, Vater, du den Erlkönig nicht?"
— Goethe "Erlkönig"
For Fiona

THE MACABRE READER

BOOK REVIEWS BY LYSETTE STEVENSON

THE BEAST OF THE HAITIAN HILLS

by Philippe Thoby-Marcelin and Pierre Marcelin translated from French by Peter C. Rhodes in 1946.

Haitian author Philippe Thoby-Marcelin in his introduction to the 1964 Time Inc edition elucidates that his inspiration to write a story about his native homeland and its religious practice of Vodou was motivated by reading American author William Seabrook's travelogue: *The Magic Island* (1932), which popularly introduced Voodoo and the concept of Zombies to the Western imagination. Enlisting the help of his brother Pierre together they crafted a supernatural comedy of errors integrating the struggles of peasant life with the richly populated spiritism of the Vodou religion.

Morin Dutilleul, a widowed and wealthy city merchant with romanticized notions of agricultural life moves to an estate in the country. With little knowledge nor respect of the villagers' cultural values, his intrusion and arrogance sets off a series of phantasmagorical events and mass hysteria. Humorous dynamics between family members of the stricken village counter the horrific dealings of the obstinate city merchant as he insults a maleficent sorcerer and cuts down a sacred tree. A frenzied chimerical beast torments the countryside while a Houngan priest is called on to help re-establish order culminating in the appearance of the venerated Vodou spirit, Master of the Cemeteries: Baron Samedi.

The Beast of the Haitian Hills pastoral landscape juxtaposed with the grotesque and tormented characters makes for an entertaining Haitian gothic read.

WINDIGO: AN ANTHOLOGY OF FACT AND FANTASTIC FICTION

edited by John Robert Colombo published by Western Producer Prairie Books, 1982.

The Windigo with over 37 spelling variations personifies the cold relentless famine of winter and the vast haunted valleys of the Canadian wilderness. Accounts ranging from folklore to fiction, poetry and artwork feature this grotesque cannibal spirit that lurks the wild Northern woods from the eastern Maritimes to the western Rockies. Once a human is possessed by its spirit, they are transformed into a lone giant with insatiable bloodlust; a creature with gnawed off lips and fingers, bulging owlish eyes and a ghoulish grimace that emits a paralyzing shriek.

John Robert Colombo's comprehensive anthology runs in chronological order starting in 1636 with Jesuit missionaries writing letters home trying to make sense of the Indigenous lore as a type of were-wolf. By the 1700's fur traders, surveyors and ethnologists were recording the frightening stories they were hearing from the Algonquian people. This in turn inspired weird fiction writers like Algernon Blackwood and August Derelth to add their own imaginations to the canon. A passage from W. H. Blake's 1915: "A Tale of the Grand Jardin," is an alluring impression of the lonesome forests of the spirit. Another fascinating excerpt comes from Morton I. Teicher's 1962 psychological study into the phenomena of Windigo Psychosis. The collection closes with a 1965 folkloric retelling by Ojibwa artist Norval Morrisseau, whose artwork is also displayed on the cover. Other work includes Ojibwa artist Carl Ray, Cree artist Jackson Beardy and woodcuts by Lynd Ward.

I came into possession of a copy after my brother attended the private library sale of a deceased professor of Anthropology. Though not an easy volume to find it should still be readily available in local libraries and always worth scouring for at one of their sales.

THE ONE THAT COMES BEFORE

by Livia Llewellyn, released 2017 by Italian horror publisher Independent Legions.

The year is 2079 and the smog polluted city of Obsidia is enduring relentless heat and humidity before the growing maelstrom. The city of millions shudders with the birthing pangs of its second Epoch.

Alex works for the Ministry as a receptionist and office assistant transcribing magical grimoires in the Library of Rare and Obscure Research Books. Alex suppresses her secret and homicidal urges with a restrained yet steady supply of liquor. By all appearances she is an outsider, living a mundane and struggling existence in a world that prays to Mother Hydra populated by Transhumanists and practitioners of Elder magic.

This novella moves at a fast and vivid pace dropping you into its immersive world with horrifying glimpses of its strange, monstrous landscape and the leviathans beneath it. The machines of the city endlessly churn for the carnivorous and complacent corporations that run it. Livia Llewellyn's Mythos writing is wholly fresh and original; weaving in visionary access to the Abyss through orgasm and death, she leaves you richer in imagination for having experienced it, wild eyed reeling and wanting for more.

Fans of Livia Llewellyn will recognize the city of Obsidia from "Her Deepness" the closing story in her stellar 2010 collection *Engines of Desire* published by Lethe Press.

CHILDREN OF THE BLACK SABBATH
by Canadian author Anne Hebert, translated from French by Carol Dunlop-Hebert in 1975.

Anne Hebert's elegant and direct prose time shifts between a mountain top shanty above a depression era Quebec village and a centuries old stone convent in Quebec City circa 1944. Sister Julie, plagued by migraines is concerned for her brother fighting overseas. She lapses into hypnagogic bouts, reliving childhood memories of satanic initiations where villagers flocked up the mountainside to partake in sabbaths, drunken revelries and orgiastic rites.

An eerie and sinister atmosphere pervades both the shanty and the nunnery. Whereas her parents are bacchanalian and neglectful ogres; the convent of the Sisters of the Precious Blood is austere and merciless. Sister Julie, both shunned and lusted after, is viewed as a yellow-eyed witch in nuns cloth. The once cloistered nunnery becomes inundated with stigmatas, possessions and a demonic perversion of immaculate conception. A beautifully rendered rural gothic nightmare of incest and depravity; blasphemy and exorcism.

Children of the Black Sabbath won the prestigious Canadian Governor General Literary award in 1975. Widely published in both hardcover and mass market paperback. In a used bookstore it is likely to be shelved with Anne Hebert's other books in the literature section rather than the more commonly considered genres of horror. In 2015, Centipede Press gave it its rightful Horror due releasing it as a limited edition (sold out) hardcover.

THE MACABRE READER, *edited by Donald A. Wollheim, dubbed "The ultimate in terrifying tales," published in 1959 by ACE and sold as a 35-cent pocket book.*

Decrepit and decaying, this fragile read is a pulp lover's dream. The cover is eye catching with its lurid font and beautifully laid out design. A titch smaller than the traditional paperback there is a novel satisfaction to the hand feel of this book.

Any of the stories in this anthology could be read elsewhere but assembled together the ghastly flow is bewitching. Each piece builds upon the other creating a grand guignol from the heaviest horror weights of Weird Tales: Bloch, Lovecraft, Zelia Bishop, Clark Ashton Smith, Robert E Howard and several more. Invasive alien slime monsters, wrathful Egyptian gods, Antarctic terror, Arkham witch cults, South American body horror, sculptural diabolism, occulted serpent worship on All Hallows night, voodoo poetry, resurrected Nordic demons and Luciferian portals; in just over two hundred pages it's a smorgasbord of frights.

This copy came into my possession from an elderly couple downsizing their books. They brought 30 boxes of dusty paperbacks for sale into my family's used bookshop, and while over half of their collection was turned away I caught my breath when I unearthed this treasure under a pile of old Westerns. Haunt your local swap meets, flea markets and garage sales for a copy of this pulp classic, as I guarantee no respectable used book seller might let their own copy go.

THE BLACK WOLF
by Galad Elflandsson, published in 1979 by Donald M. Grant, lavishly illustrated throughout by Randy Broecker, limited to 1000 copy hardcover print run with a second run of paperback editions in 1980 by Centaur Press.

Rhode Island publisher Donald M Grant read the manuscript to Galad Elflandsson's collection, *The Exile & Other Tales of Carcosa*, and he was particularly interested in the novella, *The Cave of the Hill Giant*. He asked Elflandsson that if he was willing to expand it by adding Lovecraftian elements, then Grant would be interested in publishing what became *The Black Wolf*.

On a summer vacation from the city, Paul Damon, is fishing and camping on the outskirts of a rural New England village when he is welcomed in by the congenial townsfolk. He becomes enveloped in their tension with the outcast, lone surviving descendant of the settlements founder and discovers an evil in the mountains that lies waiting as roving packs of wolves launch twilight attacks on the villagers. Witchcraft, ancient Mesopotamian gods, ghost pirates, werewolves and the Necronomicon fill out this eldritch adventure tale with the rural cosmic horror of Lovecraft and the guns blazing teeth gnashing fisticuff action of Robert E Howard. *The Black Wolf* with its fantastically eerie Randy Broecker artwork is a classic throwback to the best of Weird Tales.

2018 saw the very limited run of Galad Elflandsson's King in Yellow collection, Tales of Carcosa, through UK publisher Cyaegha Press.

CREATURES OF CLAY AND OTHER STORIES OF THE MACABRE
by Stephen Sennitt, published under the imprint A Diagonal Book by Headpress in 2003.

This collection of verbosely morbid vignettes were originally published in horror-themed zines and small presses. Nightmare narratives are unfinished and flow into the next story creating a kind of dissonance and the accumulation of these short ghoulish works have a narcotic effect. A veritable gallery of terrors: Monsters, grave robbers, Vampires, Werewolves and cursed dolls. Rot, decay and all manner of transgressions. Unsettling drawings by artist Sean Madden accentuate the sensation that while reading this you need to take a shower.

I first read this collection while working on a theatre production in British Columbia. At the end of the night I walked through the woods to a cabin I slept in nestled beneath tall fir trees that creaked and brushed against the tin roof. I propped myself up exhausted from the day and opened this book to decompress and distract myself from the hectic production period. With the amber glow of the bedside lamp contrasting against the red curtains and unfinished plywood walls I felt like the room was sinking as I disappeared into a hypnotic gaze of horrors culminating in nightmares that failed to relinquish with the sunrise.

Stephen Sennitt is also the author of the superb anthology *Ghastly Terror! The Horrible History of Horror Comics from pre-code classics to Skywald.*

TAAQTUMI: AN ANTHOLOGY OF ARCTIC HORROR STORIES
compiled by Neil Christopher, published 2019 by Inhabit Media based in Iqaluit, Nunavut.

Taaqtumi translates from Inuktitut to English as "in the dark" and the authors, both Indigenous and non-Indigenous, who live in the Northwest Territories or Nunavut personally experience that pure darkness on the tundra and the constant push for survival as a part of daily life. This unique perspective grounds these stories with a naturalism amidst the unnatural circumstances that makes the frights seep in like the bitter cold.

Shadow creatures stalk a child walking home from school in a blizzard. A man seeks vengeance against a demonic beast. A spectral doorway on the tundra invites in malevolence. Cannibalism on a trap line, a mother protecting her child from a hungry polar bear. Villagers fight back zombies and lone survivors from a viral outbreak encounter a strange doctor tempting them with salvation. The closing story, "Strays," follows a troubled mobile vet as she works in a makeshift garage operating room caring for sled dogs, it is a gruesome and gutting psych-thriller.

Inhabit Media seeks to record and preserve the oral traditions of Inuit culture, while also making it widely accessible through print. The stories in *Taaqtumi* have either a modern setting or a speculative/post-apocalyptic angle; weaving Inuit Animism and mythological storytelling into a contemporary context. As just a slim chap book it is a tantalizing glimpse into the supernatural and true to life horrors of the North.

ABERRANT VISIONS

FILM REVIEWS BY TOM GOLDSTEIN

**THE DEATH OF
DICK LONG** (2019)
Starring: Michael Abbott, Jr.,
Andre Hyland, Julia Newcomb,
Sarah Baker, et. al.
Director: Daniel Scheinert
Writer: Billy Chew
Running time: 100 minutes

November (2017)

 A couple of good ole boys unceremoniously drop their profusely bleeding bandmate at the emergency entrance of their local hospital before hightailing it away.

This backwoods ballad, set in rural Alabama, has its way with Deep South stereotypes — with 21st Century twists. The cops, for example, are a bit slow-witted and quite overweight with a fondness for baked goods. But the chief is a woman as is the main investigating officer.

The cause of Dick Long's fatal injury is revealed midway through the movie. It's shocking and disgusting, which explains why Long's buddies, Zeke and Earl, skedaddle the way they did, as well as their attempts to cover up their connection.

Some might find it to be bloody hilarious.

The movie's tone is low-key, which may actually be its strength. *The Death of Dick Long* may be easily dismissed as plain dumb. But the writing and characterization make it a lot smarter than some might think.

NOVEMBER (2017)
Starring: Rea Lest,
Jorgen Liik, et al.
Director: Rainer Sarnet
Writer: Rainer Sarnet
Running time: 115 minutes

 Based on a bestselling novel by Andrus Kivirahk, this 2017 Estonian film is steeped in Estonian folklore. Early on, viewers are introduced to the Kratt, wandering spirits with the work ethic of border collies and who take corporeal form through the assembly off tree branches, scrap metal and whatever else may be handy.

There are ghosts who parade in — they don't fly — wearing formal uniforms and are feted with hardy meals, even though the local villagers can barely feed themselves.

On the human side, there's a romantic triangle involving peasant girl Liina who's in love with peasant boy Hans who has a thing

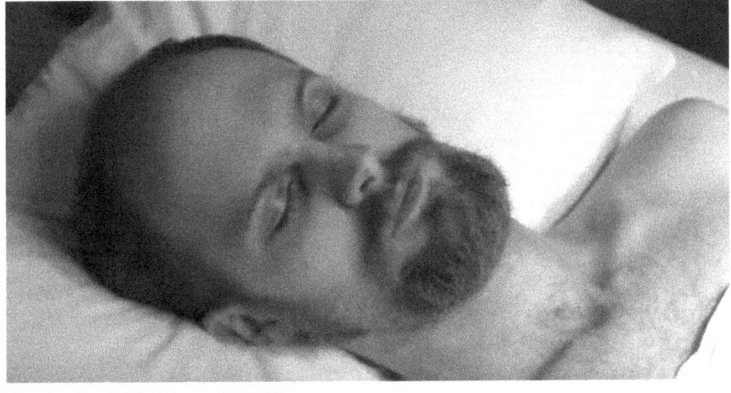

The Death of Dick Long (2019)

for a young German baroness who, well, is a damsel who periodically needs to be rescued from the distress of a sleepwalking on a mansion roof. A full moon may have something to do with the royal's nocturnal wanderings.

Shot in stunning black & white, November is a feast for the eyes with solid story-telling.

The dialogue is in Estonian and German, with English subtitles.

Satanic Panic (2019)

THE NIGHTINGALE (2018)
Director: Jennifer Kent
Writer: Jennifer Kent
Starring: Aisling Franciosi, Sam Claflin, Baykali Ganambarr
Running Time: 136 minutes

 A young Irish convict hires an Aborigine tracker to run down the British soldiers who raped her and murdered her husband and infant child in 19th century Australia.

Neither as lurid as the *I Spit on Your Grave* movies, nor as dumb as the Jennifer Garner vehicle Peppermint, this female revenge tale plays on a broader socio-political landscape than *A Vigilante*, starring Olivia Wilde.

Bleak, bloody and brutal, *The Nightingale* is not for the squeamish ... or those with a white male superiority complex.

SATANIC PANIC (2019)
Director: Chelsea Stardust
Writers: Grady Hendrix, Ted Geohagen
Starring: Rebecca Romijn, Hayley Griffith
Running Time: 85 minutes

A 22-year-old cancer survivor hits the road of her new life delivering pizzas on a Vespa. When she's stiffed for a tip at a mansion, she's determined to get the extra cash but has to fend off a suburban satanic cult in sudden need of a sacrificial virgin after the intended offering is caught losing her eligibility.

Satanic Panic is not particularly scary or creepy, but it's breezily paced with more than a few laughs.

ANYA (2019)
Starring: Anthony Aguilar, Ali Anh
Directed by: Jacob Akira Okada, Carylanna Taylor
Written by: Carylanna Taylor, Jacob Akira Okada
Running time: 80 minutes

 A young New York couple has difficulty conceiving a child. Genetic testing provides an unexpected explanation.

ANYA is low-key sci-fi. There are no monsters or bad guys, no sense of foreboding or dread. The "evil" has to do with how certain cultures — and society as a whole — treat their members.

But it is thought provoking. The genetics-based science in the movie is probably quite accurate, given the raft of PhDs listed in the closing credits.

A very human experience.

THE GOLDEN GLOVE (2019)
Starring: Jonas Dassler, Margarete Tiesel, Adam Bousdoukos
Directed by: Fatih Akin
Written by: Fatih Akin, from the novel by Heinz Strunk
Running time: 115 minutes

 Let's get this out of the way. This German-language film has nothing to do with boxing.

Rather it's a fictionalized account of Fritz Honka, who murdered and dismembered four women in Hamburg during the early 1970s and hid some of the body parts in his apartment.

The Golden Glove is the name of the dive where Honka, a suave and sophisticated ladies man in his mind only, hung out.

This is not a Hollywood movie by any stretch. The atmosphere and characters are as grimy and unappealing as the titular bar.

It's comparable to the 2003 award-winning American film *Monster*, starring Charlize Theron.

LET THE CORPSES TAN
(2017)
Starring: Elina Lowensohn, Stephane Ferrara, Bernie Bonvoisin
Directed by: Helene Cattet, Bruno Forzani
Written by: Helene Cattet, Bruno Forzani
Running time: 92 minutes.

A gang of gold thieves holes up at a sun-drenched Mediterranean island retreat. Their attempts to lay low are interrupted when people show up, including a pair of motorcycle cops.

This 2017 French-Belgium production plays like a contemporary spaghetti western. It's an homage to Sergio Leone, who catapulted Clint Eastwood to international stardom. It features lots of zoom-in closeups, including teeth clenched around a cheroot.

Ya gotta love the title. The movie's pretty good, too.

THE WILD BOYS (2017)
Starring: Pauline Lorillard,

Vilama Pons, Diane Rouxel, Anael Snoek, Mathilde Warnier
Directed by: Bertrand Mandico
Written by: Bertrand Mandico
Running time: 110 minutes

In this 2017 French adventure/fantasy a group of adolescent boys is sent to an isolated tropical island after committing a heinous crime.

Left to their own devices, the group ends up taking a Lou Reed-style walk on the wild side as the island's lush vegetation and magical powers and transforms them.

A highly atmospheric piece of cinema.

LUZ (2018)
Starring: Luana Velis, Johannes Benecke, Jan Bluthardt
Directed by: Tilman Singer
Written by: Tilman Singer
Running time: 70 minutes

Followed by a demon, a young cabbie staggers into a police precinct and spins a fascinating tale to a police psychiatrist.

This is an in-your-face, highly original piece of film-making. To borrow from — and butcher — Buffalo Springfield's *For What It's Worth*, there's something happening here, but what it is ain't exactly clear. … hey, what's that sound?

Yeah, the used of sound in *Luz* is amazing and may be nothing you've ever experienced.

A German production, *Luz* is well worth its 70 minutes, even if you come away wondering WTF you just watched.

MARLINA THE MURDERER IN FOUR ACTS (2017)
Starring: Marsha Timothy, Egy Fedly
Directed by: Mouly Surya
Written by: Rama Adi, Garin Nugroho, Mouly Surya
Running time: 93 minutes

Marlina is a young widow who lives alone in rural Indonesia with the mummified corpse of her husband. She is confronted by an outlaw

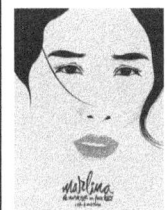

gang leader who calmly informs her his crew will be by a bit later for a home-cooked meal and she will be, uhm, dessert.

The gang and their boss show up and eat the last meal they'll ever have. The boss gets his just desserts.

Marlina tries to go to the police, but not even the severed head she carries around in a satchel can get their attention.

Done as a contemporary western, this 2017 movie is a low-key, dryly humorous — if somewhat grisly — commentary on sexual politics in Indonesia.

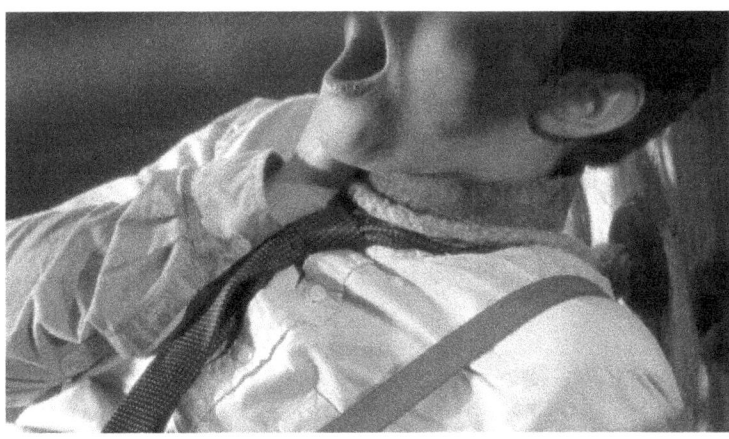

The Wild Boys (2017)

CONTRIBUTORS

DAVID BOWMAN is an illustrator, painter, and software developer. He lives with his family and ancient cat in Fishers, Indiana.

SHIKHAR DIXIT'S fiction has appeared in such venues as *Dark Regions, Strange Horizons, Not One of Us*, The Darker Side (edited by John Pelan), and several Barnes & Nobles anthologies. He lives in the darkest heart of New Jersey. To learn more, visit SlipOfThePen.com

STEVE DUFFY'S short fiction has appeared in magazines and anthologies in Europe and North America. His most recent collection of weird stories, *The Moment Of Panic*, was published in 2013; it includes the International Horror Guild award-winning short story, "The Rag-and-Bone Men." In 2016 Steve won a Shirley Jackson Award for his story "Even Clean Hands Can Do Damage," originally published in Supernatural Tales 30. He lives and works in North Wales, one of the settings for "White Noise In A White Room."

INNA EFFRESS is a former speechwriter who emigrated from Ukraine to the U.S. as a child. Her short fiction has been nominated for the Pushcart Prize and has appeared in publications such as *Santa Monica Review, The Wrong, Nightscript III, Spirits Unwrapped*, and *The Best Horror of the Year Volume 10*, among others. She has a story in *Noir Nation*, issue 9, and in Tartarus Press' 30th-anniversary anthology. Inna writes for ThinkWatts, an organization that brings economic and educational opportunities to inner-city youth. She tutors homeless students in Los Angeles through School on Wheels.

TOM GOLDSTEIN spent about 35 years working in various capacities in newsrooms of major newspapers across Canada — as a reporter, editor and a couple of extracurricular stints as a music or video reviewer. He has never — and still does not — consider himself a critic. Rather he's just a guy who really likes movies, with a particular interest in "different."

ORRIN GREY is a skeleton who likes monsters as well as the author of several spooky books. His stories of ghosts, monsters, and sometimes the ghosts of monsters can be found in dozens of anthologies, including Ellen Datlow's *Best Horror of the Year*. He resides in the suburbs of Kansas City and watches lots of scary movies. You can visit him online at orringrey.com.

VINCE HAIG is an illustrator, designer, and author. You can visit Vince at his website: barquing.com

JOHN LANGAN is the author of two novels and four collections of stories. For his second novel, *The Fisherman*, he received the Bram Stoker and This Is Horror awards. He's one of the founders of the Shirley Jackson awards. Currently, he reviews horror and dark fantasy for Locus magazine. He lives in New York's Mid-Hudson Valley with his wife, younger son, and a tiny Godzilla who guards his writing desk.

SUZAN PALUMBO lives in Canada. Originally from Trinidad and Tobago, she is an ESL teacher and Gothic literature enthusiast. Her stories are often inspired by clashes of culture and the horror that lurks in the gap between expectations and reality. Her work has been published by *PseudoPod, Fireside Quarterly, PodCastle* and *Anathema: Spec from the Margins* among others. Her full bibliography can be found at suzanpalumbo.wordpress.com

IAN ROGERS is the author of the award-winning collection, Every House Is Haunted. A novelette from the collection, "The House on Ashley Avenue," was a finalist for the Shirley Jackson Award. His work has been selected for several "best of the year" anthologies, and many of his stories have been optioned for film and television. Ian lives with his wife in Peterborough, Ontario. For more information, visit ianrogers.ca.

NABEN RUTHNUM lives and writes in Toronto. As Nathan Ripley, he's published two thrillers with Atria / Simon & Schuster.

LYSETTE STEVENSON is a stage manager with a rural outdoor equestrian theatre company and a second generation bookseller. She lives in British Columbia.

SIMON STRANTZAS is the author of five collections of short fiction, including *Nothing is Everything* (Undertow Publications, 2018), and editor of a number of anthologies, including *Year's Best Weird Fiction, Vol. 3*. Combined, he's been a finalist for four Shirley Jackson Awards, two British Fantasy Awards, and the World Fantasy Award. His fiction has appeared in numerous annual best-of anthologies, and in venues such as *Nightmare, The Dark*, and *Cemetery Dance*. In 2014, his edited anthology, *Aickman's Heirs*, won the Shirley Jackson Award. He lives with his wife in Toronto, Canada.

STEVE TOASE writes regularly for Fortean Times and Folklore Thursday. His fiction has recently appeared in *Nightmare Magazine, Shadows & Tall Trees 8, Nox Pareidolia*, and *Lackington's*. Three of his stories have been republished in Ellen Datlow's Best Horror of the Year anthologies. His first short story collection *To Drown In Dark Water* is due out from Undertow Publications in 2021. Steve lives in Munich, and likes old motorbikes and vintage cocktails. You can keep up to date with his work via his Patreon www.patreon.com/stevetoase

NATHANIEL WINTER-HEBERT operates from a studio cabin tucked into the wilds of Québec. He presides his wizardly duties as art director of *The Ghastling* and the folk-horror magazine *Hellebore*. He spends his day concocting all manners of visual editorial curiosities and more: winterhebert.com

SAM HEIMER is a Philadelphia area Illustrator, and Designer. Follow him on Instagram @Sam_Heimer